BUCK ROGERS #2
That Man on Beta

A NOVEL BY
Addison E. Steele

BASED ON A STORY AND
TELEPLAY BY
Bob Shane

A DELL BOOK

Published by
Dell Publishing Co., Inc.
1 Dag Hammarskjold Plaza
New York, New York 10017

This work is based on the teleplay
by Bob Shane

Dell ® TM 681510, Dell Publishing Co., Inc.

ISBN: 0-440-10948-5

Printed in the United States of America
First printing—January 1979

CHAPTER 1.

The threat of invasion had been met. The Draconian fleet had been whipped, its storm-force destroyed by Earth's defense squadron—a squadron fighting under the command of Colonel Wilma Deering, and using the aggressive, free-swinging tactics developed on the American frontier seven hundred years before and updated to the needs of the twenty-fifth century by Captain Buck Rogers.

The storm-force destroyed, Earth's defense perimeter secured, Draconia's main force swung through a wide space-orbit and fled back to the boundaries of its home empire, fled like a whipped cur with its tail between its legs.

The flagship—also known as the *Draconia*—had been blown to bits. The Princess Ardala and her would-be consort, Kane, had escaped with their lives—barely—in a tiny, sealed pod. Now they would face the wrath of the Emperor Draco.

Not that the Draconian Empire would rest while the bitter gall of defeat still burned in the heart of its emperor. Draco had other wars to fight, other enemies to subdue. But Earth's turn would come once again, of that there need be no doubt.

And the Princess Ardala and her ruthless, oily, treacherous suitor would surely place themselves in the forefront of Draconia's ceaseless war of conquest.

Meanwhile, life on Earth returned to normal—or what passed for normal in these closing decades of the twenty-fifth century. The Inner City ruled Earth in splendor while much of the planet's surface remained a seething, radioactive wasteland where savages and mutants prowled the ruins of a long-ago civilization whose politicians and militarists had led it to Armageddon.

The defense squadron continued to train and maneuver under the guidance of its brilliant commander, Wilma Deering. And Colonel Deering continued to fret over the conduct of Captain William "Buck" Rogers, that strange revenant of the twentieth century whose return to Earth and enlistment in the space force had brought with it both the sharpest flying and fighting skills in the known universe—and the thorniest problems in personal relationships in Colonel Deering's distinguished career.

At the Inner City defense squadron spacefield, Buck Rogers' sleek starfighter flashed in for a landing. Its powerful engines and advanced guidance systems were as far beyond the crude spacecraft of Buck's youth as those spacecraft were beyond the motorized boxkites of the Wright Brothers.

The starfighter rockets were fitted with computers of a complexity and speed that would have set a twentieth-century electronics engineer to gibbering with mystification and delight. And

Buck Rogers was by no means averse to letting those computers handle all of the routine operation and checking procedures of his space fighter. But when it came to the crunch, Buck flew his own ship.

He remembered the legend of the first moon-landing, back in the dusty days of his own twentieth century. The lem had been fitted with the fastest and most complex computers available in *those* long-ago days—but when it came down to the ultimate, life-or-death seconds as the module skimmed over a rock-strewn plain, desperately seeking a smooth landing area in which to set down before its fast-dwindling fuel supply ran out, it was the astronauts, Buz Aldrin and Neil Armstrong, who took command and brought the *Eagle* in for a safe landing.

This was the lesson that Buck Rogers had carried from the twentieth century to the twenty-fifth: that all of mankind's creations could amplify and assist him in his efforts. But no machine could take the place of a trained, intelligent, determined human being.

Now Buck set his starfighter down on the tarmac and gave control of the rocket to its computers. They could monitor its condition, shut down its power systems, signal to maintenance crews for whatever parts needed servicing before the craft was next called upon to blast into the black void beyond Earth on a mission that would probably . . . most probably . . . involve only routine training and patrol responsibilities.

As Buck strode away from the starfighter his crew chief trotted toward the rocket. "Captain

Rogers," the chief called. "Captain Rogers, I need your condition readouts, sir."

Concentrating on whatever thoughts occupied his mind, Buck hardly even heard the crew chief's words.

"Captain Rogers," the chief called again. "I need your closing fuel reading, ammo report, computer readouts. . . ."

Buck half-heard the chief. Without breaking his stride he jerked one thumb back over his shoulder, indicating the starfighter with its built-in computer circuitry. The gesture said as plainly as words could have done, "Get that from the computers, chief. That's what they're for."

Grumbling, the chief gave up on trying to stop Buck and trotted off toward the starfighter itself. Captain Rogers was right, he knew—the information he needed was all available in the spacecraft's data-banks and condition-circuits. He undogged the pilot's hatch of the rocket and tapped the first of a series of access codes into the ship's master computer.

Buck disappeared from the spacefield itself, striding purposefully into the monorail station that served the field. He sank into a round mass that instantly adjusted itself to fit Buck's body shape and his body temperature, and gazed abstractedly from the window of the car as the monorail whizzed from the spacefield into the heart of the Inner City itself.

The ultramodern buildings that flanked the monorail line had held Buck's fascinated attention the first time he'd seen them after recovering from his five-hundred-years' orbit in suspended animation. Their soaring towers, shimmering domes, gracefully swooping roadways, and splendid open plazas had dazzled eyes grown accustomed to the grime and pollution of twentieth-century Chicago, Buck Rogers' home town.

But by now the glories of the Inner City were as familiar to Buck as were the sun-baked buildings of Houston or the whispering palmettos of Cape Canaveral to the astronauts of an earlier age. When the monorail glided smoothly to a halt at his stop, Buck climbed from the sleek car, made his way through glowing white corridors, and took a final familiar turn; doors opened automatically, slid inconspicuously into the wall.

He strode into a spotless, white-walled anteroom.

In the center of the room stood a sleekly functional desk fabricated of the same glowing white material as the room itself. Behind the desk, seated on a white swivel chair, was a vaguely humanlike figure also of the same glowing white. It was as if the whole environment—room, furniture, figure— had been carved from a single shimmering block of perfect white marble. Buck was the only bit of color in the room.

He stood in the center of the room, the door whispered shut behind him. The figure behind the desk turned its head toward him, spoke in a remarkably natural-sounding voice, for all that the sounds were generated electronically under the command of the figure's own computer.

"He's busy," the figure said.

Buck turned aside and found a seat for himself. He returned his attention to the white figure. It was a secretarial robot. For all that its functions were impersonal and administrative, extensive psychological testing of Inner City executives had shown that they could work most effectively with robots cast into forms at least suggestive of human beings.

The secretarial robot was a Lisa 5 model, and without being female in any biological sense, its fabrication was in lines whose grace was suggestive of a young woman and its programming gave it—or *her*—the mannerisms and voice of an intelligent, educated young woman of an earlier century.

The robot looked expectantly at Buck Rogers.

"I'll wait," Buck grated impatiently.

"I don't see you on his calendar," the robot answered. Although she had the information in her data-banks, she politely went through the motions of examining a desk calendar, her gracefully formed mechanical fingers tracing the day's schedule as her electronic visual scanners tracked across the orderly notations.

"I don't see you on his calendar," the mechanical, yet pleasantly feminine, voice repeated.

"I'm not on his calendar," Buck grinned, "I'm on his bench."

The robot-receptionist sat for a moment in puzzled silence. If she had had the right relays and capacitors, she might have frowned in concentration. "I can't quite compute that, Captain

Rogers," she said at last. "Perhaps there's something wrong with my circuits."

"You've got a great set of circuits, kid," Buck wisecracked.

The robot scanned her anatomy uncertainly. "Thank you."

"Of course," Buck said more to himself than the Lisa 5, "everything looks good to a guy after five hundred years, just about."

The Lisa 5 turned back to her work. She pulled a sheet of paper from a slot in her desk, slipped it into the futuristic equivalent of what Buck would have recognized, in his own era, as a super-typewriter with advanced data-storage and -retrieval circuits built into its chassis, and began to type. Her fingers moved faster than Buck's eyes could follow; they appeared to turn into a translucent white blur. Almost before she had started typing, the Lisa 5 pulled the completed page from her typewriter and slipped it into another slot in her desk. With an almost inaudible whoosh the sheet of paper disappeared into the desk and was carried away to its destination.

"Who taught you to type?" Buck asked the female robot. "Some kind of speed demon?"

"Demons are an unscientific superstition unsubstantiated by any objectively verifiable evidence," the robot answered coolly. "Typing programs are coded into the circuitry of all Lisa 5 secretarial robots. We come from the factory with the capability already present in us."

Buck crossed the room and leaned familiarly across the desk. In a low voice he suggested,

"Maybe sometime after work we could go out for a can of 3-in-One oil." While he held the robot's attention by speaking, he surreptitiously flicked on the intercom button built into the control panel of her desk.

Before the robot could respond to Buck's invitation, a panel slid smoothly aside in the wall behind her. Beyond the reception room lay an elaborate office. In it stood the science wizard of the Inner City, the man who had first evaluated Buck on the spaceman's return to the city from the Draconian space fleet that had found his ship in its five-hundred-year orbit. On that occasion Huer had sympathized with the astronaut, sided with him, and helped him through his trial with the Inner City computer council.

Now the brilliant, ascetic Huer peered into the outer chamber from his office. "Lisa, what's going on out there?" he addressed the secretarial robot.

Before the robot could answer, Buck cut in. "Dr. Huer, it's all my fault. Can I see you for a minute?"

"Rogers. Of course. You know my door is always open to you."

"If I can find it," Buck grinned.

"Come in," the aged scientist gestured, "come in."

As the young spaceman entered the inner office, the wall panel slid closed behind him, leaving the Lisa 5 alone once more at her desk. With soundless efficiency the robot slipped another blank sheet of paper into her typewriter and poised slim mechanical fingers above the keyboard. Before she began typing, however, she swiveled her head in the direction of the inner office, where Buck Rogers had disappeared. "Three and one oil?" the robot murmured to herself. "Why not say four oil instead?"

CHAPTER 2.

Inside the office of the science wizard, Buck Rogers and Dr. Huer settled into comfortable seats. "I hope you're thriving on our hospitality, Captain Rogers," the scientist said.

"Hey, great," Buck exclaimed. "It's terrific, Doc. I like the twenty-fifth-century chow. The Vinol's tops—better than the bubbly I could afford on air force pay back in the 1980s."

"But," Dr. Huer peered seriously into the younger man's face, "you have a complaint, eh?"

"It's . . . not quite a complaint," Buck conceded. "More of a request, I guess. It's that—well, Doc, there's more to life than food and drink. . . ."

Dr. Huer smiled knowingly. "Oh, so *that's* it. Well, that's understandable. It's been five hundred years. Just ask any of the men in the defense squadron for directions to the Palace of Pleasure."

"No, no, no," Buck snorted. "I don't mean that. You don't have to worry about me in that department. I can take care of myself."

Dr. Huer raised his eyebrows. "Are you sure that's such a good idea for a grown man, Buck?"

Buck Rogers sat, puzzled for a moment. Then his breath exploded. "No, no, no!" he repeated.

14

"*That* isn't what I meant, either. Dr. Huer, what I mean is this—"

The aged scientist leaned forward expectantly.

"I need a leave of absence," Buck went on. "Not just from flying duty—I'd talk to Wilma if that were the only thing. No, I have to leave the Inner City, at least for a while. I need to go out into Anarchia. I've got to—to find out what happened to my family. I've got to know if I have anyone left on Earth. Of course my immediate family were all gone centuries ago. But do I have descendants anywhere on Earth? Or off it, for that matter—anywhere in the galaxy?"

The jocular atmosphere of a few minutes earlier had disappeared. Buck strode around Dr. Huer's office like a restless lion patrolling the bars of its cage. "Do you know what isolation is, Doc? What we used to call alienation in my day? A sense of not belonging, of being cut off from all of humankind? I have to find out if I have a blood connection to any living, breathing human being."

Buck returned to his comfortable chair and slumped into it, his shoulders sagging and his head downcast. "I feel so . . . so . . . alone, Doc."

"I understand," Huer nodded. "It must be very difficult coming from a different time and place. Suddenly finding yourself in a new world, half a millennium out of your own time."

"It's funny," Buck said, but not with any sign of amusement. "If this were some different planet and I couldn't get home, somehow that wouldn't be quite as frustrating. I'd know that my own people were still alive, might still be alive. Somehow, somewhere.

"But this isn't a different place. My home was only 30 or 40 miles from here. I mean, 50 or 60 kilometers. I've got to see it. What's left of it. Or even what *isn't* left of it."

"That could be very dangerous," Dr. Huer put in. "It isn't just kilometers—miles—that are at stake. Once you pass beyond the Inner City's dome, we can't offer you protection. Anything could happen out there, Buck."

"But I have to do it," Buck dissented. "What I have to do is track down my—I don't know. It's not my roots I want to trace. It's sort of . . . my sprouts." As Buck's irrepressible humor broke through his seriousness, he found himself unwillingly grinning again.

"But the last time you went out there—when we mistakenly exiled you from the Inner City, Buck—you found your family's graves. You wouldn't leave Anarchia until you found them. Isn't that so?"

"Yes," Buck conceded. "My parents were dead and buried in old Chicago, what you now call Anarchia. And so were my brother and my sister. But maybe *someone* survived. A cousin, a niece or nephew. And if someone survived the holocaust back in the twentieth century, they might have had children. And *they* might have had children. I'd have living relatives now. For all I know, *you* might be my great-great-great-whatever, my nephew, Doc. I need to *know!*"

The old scientist smiled at the notion that the young man opposite him might be an ancestor of his. Then a more serious expression replaced the smile on his face. "Buck," he said earnestly, "I can't let you go out there. The odds are too slim. And you're too valuable to the Inner City. If only for your knowledge of the Earth of the twentieth century. But beyond that, you're such a natural starfighter pilot. We can't afford to let you risk your life."

"You let me risk my life fighting the Draconians," Buck snapped back angrily. "I'm not too valuable for that risk, am I!"

"But that was for the common good of all," Huer almost pleaded. "That was a risk taken for all of Earth—I might even say, for all of civilization."

"So what's my family," Buck asked with a combination of bitterness and wry humor, "chopped liver?"

Huer's response was a look of bafflement.

Buck tried more directly: "Are you going to let me go or aren't you?"

Dr. Huer shook his head. "I can't take the chance of having you killed or captured by a pack of savages or mutants, Buck. I don't suppose it would help if I said that I have your own welfare at heart, as well as the needs of the community."

"No sir, it wouldn't," Buck conceded. He stood up and moved toward the exit. "Thank you, sir. Good-bye."

As the sliding panel that served for a doorway opened before Buck, Dr. Huer took note of the determined set of the younger man's jaw. A seasoned judge of human behavior, a careful reader of expressions in people's voices and in their body language, Huer could tell that Buck Rogers was not going to take no for an answer—that the closing of the office panel behind the spaceman was by no means the closing of the matter under discussion.

As Buck strode angrily past the typing desk in the reception office, the Lisa 5 addressed him. "Buck, about that four oil, I've never heard of—"

He was gone, totally ignoring the secretarial robot's words.

"Huh," the Lisa 5 commented to herself, "five hundred years old, is he? Must be senile by this time!"

Not long after, Buck was at the defense squadron spacefield at the edge of the Inner City dome. Despite his personal problems, while he remained the guest of the Inner City he would always carry out his duties as a rocket pilot bearing the rank of captain in the defense squadron.

The other squadron pilots were gathered, along with Buck, for a technical briefing by their commander, in which she explained to them the features of a new energy-booster system that power engineers had finished installing, just an hour before, on their starfighters.

The pilots included women and men, and members of all the races of Earth. In this regard, at least, the civilization of the twenty-fifth century had not merely recovered the ground lost in the ravaging Third World War half a millennium before, but had made reality of the idealistic goals of the old civilization.

The defense squadron commander, Colonel Wilma Deering, was at the end of her briefing and about to open the floor for questions from her subordinates. "So the new energy pods,"

Colonel Deering concluded, "will enable our
fighters to go into star warp at least for limited
periods."

Most of the pilots remained silent as they assim-
ilated the new information, but Buck Rogers
responded with a sharp question. "What are the
outside limits on speed and duration?"

"I think I already covered that point, Captain
Rogers," Wilma Deering replied. In her off-duty
hours she was clearly one of the most beautiful,
feminine, and desirable women in the Inner City
—but on duty she was all crisp military efficiency.
"The council has ordered us not to exceed 42,000
D.E.T. or to remain in star warp for longer than
140 S.S. seconds."

"That isn't exactly what I asked, Colonel," Buck
shot back. "That's a policy directive from the
political leadership. I was asking the technical
limitations of the new gear."

The eyes of commander and pilot locked in an
angry, sparking duel of wills. The relationship
between Colonel Deering, commander, and Captain Rogers, pilot, was difficult enough. Rogers
was the most skilled and daring of the defense
squadron's spacemen, an incalculable asset to the
protection of the Inner City. But he was head-
strong, independent, and not amenable to discipline.

If that dilemma wasn't tough enough to deal
with, there was the similarly difficult relationship
between Wilma Deering and Buck Rogers.

Well, there wasn't time to deal with the com-
plexities of such matters now. "The answer I gave

you is the official position of the defense squadron," she answered coldly.

Captain Rogers clearly remained unplacated, but before he could speak again the briefing room was jolted by the strident sounds of a siren's wail. After a few seconds of ear-splitting wailing, the siren dropped away and a voice spoke through the loudspeaker. "Code A," the voice announced urgently, "Code A. Radar reports unidentified blip. Fighter squadron will scramble at once. Scramble at once. Repeat—Code A, Code A."

Colonel Deering pressed a control stud, answered the intercom voice. "Squadron commander speaking. Code A received and acknowledged. We're on our way."

Within seconds the constant training of almost-daily drill scrambles of the defense squadron came to the fore. Pilots sprinted across the spacefield tarmac and vaulted into fighter rockets already warming up under the quick response of razor-sharp ground crews.

With a massive roar as rocket engines blasted the fighters off their launching pads and into the sky above the Inner City, the starfighter squadron zoomed away from the spaceport.

Colonel Deering radioed back to base. "Squadron approaching C Sector. No other spacecraft in range of visual sighting or instrument detection. What are our instructions?"

"Suggest you scan coordinates 14-40, C Sector," the crackling voice of ground control responded. "We request you attempt visual sighting of unidentified blip and report findings at once."

"14-40," Colonel Deering responded, "C Sector. Check, ground control. Here we go."

Wilma Deering adjusted the controls on a glowing, flickering panel of electronic scanners and computer readouts that all but filled the compact cockpit of her powerful starfighter. On an eerily glowing telescreen she adjusted the coordinates to match those radioed from ground control and punched a read-in button to send the information to the starfighter's master astrogation computer.

"Defense squadron," she radioed all her pilots, "set astrogation computers to coordinates 14-40, C Sector. Execute 18 degree turn. Ready—mark!"

In a display of precision team flying that would have set the navy's Blue Devils of Buck Rogers' time agape with envy, the starfighter squadron swooped through a graceful maneuver, zeroing in on the space coordinates dictated by their commander. At the identical instant there appeared a faint dot dead in the center of the glowing telescreen in the cockpit of every fighter.

"Colonel Deering," a pilot's voice came over the intership radio, "I have visual contact with target at screen center."

Wilma Deering nodded. "Good. I scan also. Any idea what it is?"

"Negative," the pilot replied.

Another pilot's voice crackled across the ether. "Can't tell from here either."

"I'll go for a closer look," Buck Rogers radioed. As usual, instead of waiting for orders he was taking the initiative in responding to a challenge from the deeps of space.

The pilots of the squadron cut their engines to

half-idle as they awaited further instructions. Colonel Deering radioed to Buck Rogers and the rest of her command: "Negative, Rogers. Cut to half power. All ships stabilize in orbit on my command. Ready—mark!"

The squadron moved in on the unfamiliar object, carried through the virtual vacuum of space by the momentum of their velocity. As they approached the object it became obvious that it was what they had all suspected: an alien spacecraft.

Again the ether snapped with the exchange of messages between Colonel Deering and the pilots in her squadron:

"I've never seen a ship like that!"

"It's not Draconian!"

"Nor Gregorian!"

"Doesn't look like a pirate ship, either!"

Suddenly the slowly drifting ship flashed into lightninglike movement. Almost before any of the Inner City's pilots could react, the alien craft was disappearing into the blackness, the glow of its power-pods the only means left by which to follow its course.

"Look," Wilma gasped, "it's going into—"

"Star warp!" Buck Rogers completed for her. "I'll follow!"

"Captain Rogers, wait!" Wilma commanded.

"If I wait we'll never know what that thing was!" Buck slapped at the controls of his star-fighter with the studied confidence of a spaceman who has spent so many hours at the controls of his ship that he could execute any maneuver blindfolded, standing on his head and with one hand tied behind his back.

Her voice rising to an angry pitch, Colonel Deering almost shouted into her radio: "Captain Rogers, I'll give the orders here! Now—"

But even as Wilma tried to call him back, Buck Rogers' ship flashed away from the rest of the defense squadron, accelerating wildly along the trail of the almost invisible alien craft. Within seconds Buck's starfighter accelerated to the maximum speed of normal matter moving within normal space. Buck's mass, like that of his ship, increased hugely. Strange distortions of both space and time swept over pilot and craft.

Then Buck threw in the switch that activated his starfighter's new booster pods, and his ship crashed the invisible barrier that separates normal three-dimensional space from the bizarre realm of the hyperuniverse where light-speed barriers are unknown and stranger phenomena occur than we can even imagine.

Buck radioed back a message, hoping that he might still get word to Wilma before his starfighter had penetrated too far into the hyperspace realm. "I see him now, Colonel. Closing in. I'm at 42,000 D.E.T. If I shove this crate up to 43 I think I can catch him. Just how safe is it to exceed 42, Colonel? No politics!"

"Captain Rogers," Wilma Deering almost screamed into her microphone, "I order you to cease star warp and return to fleet at once!"

"Just one more minute," Buck grated.

"I'll have you court-martialed! Rejoin fleet now!"

Buck glared at his communicator, reached his right hand as if to set a switch, then simply shrugged and stretched out his left hand instead for the booster-pod-deactivator switch.

Inside the alien ship, a pilot sat at the control panel in a large, well-lighted area. Unlike the starfighters of Earth's defense squadron, this alien ship was huge. Instead of a cramped cockpit built to hold a single pilot, it had a bridge large enough to accommodate a full complement of specialists.

And unlike its enigmatically designed exterior, the alien ship's interior showed a style of fittings and equipment that Colonel Deering and her starfighter pilots would have recognized instantly, had they seen it.

It was Draconian.

"We've lost the Earth ship," the Draconian pilot grunted into a microphone. "He pursued us into warp space, but then for some reason he seemed to drop back into ordinary, sir."

The voice coming back through the radio seethed with fury. "You were not supposed to lose it, you idiot! *Ach*, that's just what I'd expect of you fools! Can't I get anyone competent to do what I tell them?"

The pilot's face grew pale with fear. "I'm sorry, Lord Kane. I thought you *wanted* me to get away from pursuit."

Although the pilot couldn't see the face of the other man, he could imagine the rage contorting the already unpleasantly beefy features of Kane.

CHAPTER 3.

At the defense squadron spaceport of the Inner City a sharply ordered formation of space pilots stood before their pacing commander. Their starfighters had been wheeled off the tarmac by ground crewmen who were even now busily refueling and servicing the rockets so they would be ready to blast off on a moment's notice when the word next came for a scramble.

Where the space pilots stood in orderly formation, Colonel Wilma Deering stopped her pacing before Captain Buck Rogers. As he stood at his full height the colonel had to peer upward into his face, but she did so not with the wilting helplessness of a soft woman. She did so with the angry expression of a military commander prepared to dress down a defiant subordinate.

"Your conduct was just what I would expect of you, Rogers! You're impetuous, insubordinate, and uncivilized!"

For long seconds she glared angrily into his square-jawed face, then she spun on her heel and strode away.

Under his breath, Buck Rogers murmured, "But I'm cute."

Half-hearing the words, Colonel Deering whirled
back to face Buck again. "Did you say something,
Rogers?"

"No, sir," the captain replied.

"And I don't find that amusing either," Colonel
Deering snapped. "You're all dismissed." She
stood with her fists on her hips for a few seconds
as the pilots broke formation, then stalked angrily
from the field.

One of the other pilots approached Buck Rogers.
"Dr. Huer put out a message, Buck. He wants to
see you, pronto."

"Check," Buck nodded.

"I wonder why she was so hard on you," another
pilot commented to Buck.

The captain grinned. "Probably because she was
right." He slapped his colleague on the arm and
strode away toward the monorail station. In a
short time he was closeted with the science wizard
of Inner City once more.

"Buck Rogers," the wizened savant spoke without preliminary, "I may be able to help you after
all."

Buck's reply was sarcastic. "Terrific, Doc. How?"

"I've programmed the master computer bank,
requesting a complete genealogical readout on
you and your family. Would you like to hear it?"

Interest kindled in Buck's eyes. "Yeah, I sure
would."

"Okay," Huer told him. "Just have a seat and
I'll summon up the data." He turned toward a
computer terminal outfitted with a microphone
and a loudspeaker. "Proceed with data readout,"
the scientist instructed the computer.

Lights blinked across the surface of the control panel, and servomechanisms whirred as data records were spun into position. "Family of Rogers, William, a.k.a. Buck," the computer's mechanical voice sounded. "Father James Rogers. Mother Edna Rogers. Brother Frank Rogers. Sister Marilyn Rogers. All died April, 1988. Cause: holocaust. Sister-in-law Ellen Rogers, wife of Frank. Died May, 1988. Cause: holocaust. No record of other relations or descendants."

The voice lapsed into silence and the whir of moving records murmured softly in the background.

"I'm sorry, Buck," the aged Dr. Huer spoke softly.

Before Buck could answer, the whirring of records gave way to another statement by the computer's electronic voice. "Further information retrieved from data-banks. Jackie Rogers, daughter of Ellen and Frank. Disappeared as of May, 1988. Last recorded address, Chicago, Illinois. Presumed dead in holocaust, but death not confirmed and may have survived in Anarchia or made way off-planet. No further data on Jackie Rogers. No record of descendants. No other known relatives of subject William 'Buck' Rogers."

"Then there's hope!" Buck's countenance lit up.

Huer shook his head. "Buck, forget it. After five hundred years, what chance is there?"

"I can't forget it, Doc. As long as there's any chance at all—" He saw the solemn look on Dr. Huer's face, thought for a while, then spoke again, bitterly. "Yes, you're right, Doc. I know that you're right. Thanks for trying."

He headed for the door of the office, ignored
the trim Lisa 5 robot in Huer's outer office,
stumbled down the corridor despondently, and
almost collided with Wilma Deering as she
emerged from the door of another facility.

The two pilots dodged, backed, and tried to
give way to each other. The performance was
almost a dance, and Buck's gloom lightened somewhat with the humor of the moment. They started
walking side by side, then repeated their encounter
by beginning simultaneously to apologize.

"I know I shouldn't have done those . . ."

"I shouldn't have been so rough on . . ."

Again they both stopped and laughed at themselves.

Wilma said, "You're not mad?"

Buck shook his head. "I deserved the chewing
out. You're not mad either?"

"No," Wilma shook her head. "Buck, I'm making
a very special dinner tonight. Euranian Clipsop
and all the trimmings." She stopped walking, faced
Buck as he also halted and turned toward her.
"Can you come, Buck? My place for an intimate
meal and . . ."

"No," Buck responded after a fraction of a
second, "I'm afraid I can't."

"You *are* mad," Wilma exclaimed.

"No, honestly, I'm not mad at all. But I just
can't make it." He shrugged helplessly. "Besides,
I don't have the faintest idea what a Clipsop is."

Wilma leaned closer so that her breath was
warm on the side of Buck's face. "Then I'll have
to teach you," she whispered.

Buck laughed. "I'll really look forward to it. But

not tonight, Wilma. Really." He leaned down and
kissed her lightly—on the forehead. "Sometime,
though," he said. "In fact, let's make it real soon
now."

He strode away, down the brightly lit corridor.
Behind him Wilma Deering stood gazing with
a mixture of annoyance, disappointment, and suspicion.

Back in his quarters, Buck at last had a chance
to switch from his flying suit—a combination of
smart military styling and purely functional life-
support systems that would have been the envy
of any twentieth-century astronaut. He stood in
the center of his room, clad only in skimpy shorts.

Looking across the room to the rack where his
twenty-fifth-century civilian clothes hung, he
spoke softly. "Twiki, would you get me that pair
of pants?"

The object of his address was a small robot. It
stood less than waist high, compared to Buck. Its
shape was a compact, stumpy one designed to
pack a maximum volume of electronic circuitry
and mechanical parts into a minimum amount of
space. Its scanners glistened beneath the clean
lights of a standard Inner City personal lodging
unit. Its movements had the humorous appearance
of a willing but not overly bright Barbary ape
reduced to mechanical form.

The robot, Twiki, became activated in response
to Buck's quiet request. It—or *he*—scuttered across
the room, tilting alternately from side to side with
each step of his stumpy legs. He reached the
clothing rack, picked up Buck's trousers, and

started back toward the spaceman with the trousers in his hands.

Halfway across the room, the robot's movements became unsteady and erratic. He hesitated, hopped forward again, tottered, and nearly fell. Finally he came to a complete halt, extending his arms with the trousers neatly folded on them, toward Buck.

"A little closer, please," the spaceman asked.

Twiki's arms moved, his scanner lenses revolved in concentration, he lifted his feet and stamped them in place, but somehow could not move forward another centimeter. He made a final, convulsive effort to complete his movement—and failed. There was a sound like a small explosion somewhere inside the robot. A shudder passed through the machine, and a puff of smoke escaped from it, as if several circuits had fused. The robot ceased all movement. The small cloud of smoke that had escaped it drifted upward, partially disappearing into the fabric of Buck's trousers.

"Hah, modern technology!" Buck grunted. He reached for the robot and took back his trousers. He slapped the cloth to clear it of fumes, then pulled the pants over his legs.

He bent to examine the robot, talking to Twiki as one would to a sick child or an injured pet while checking the extent of its hurts. "My car used to do this in the old days," Buck muttered. He opened a slightly charred panel on the torso of the robot, reached inside, and examined the wiring within. "I wonder if you can jump-start a robot."

Obviously, Buck did something wrong. There

was another crackling sound, and another puff of smoke rose toward the ceiling.

Buck Rogers felt a jolt of electricity as the energy in the immobilized power cells drained— fortunately for Buck, only partially—from its interior, through the shorted circuits and into him. Even the partial dose of the robot's energy supply sent the spaceman across the room with a jolt. He was dazed into semi-consciousness by the double effect of the electric shock and the unexpected flight across his room.

"Get off me!" a muffled, mechanical-sounding voice said.

Still partially dazed, Buck looked around for the source.

"You're sitting on me!" The mechanical voice sounded annoyed.

Comprehending at last, Buck pushed himself to his feet and retrieved the object he'd unknowingly sat on. It was a small rectangular box with sides of polished, plasticlike material. The insides of the box were not themselves visible through the tinted, dark plastic that surrounded them.

But a series of indicator lights covered most of the interior of one surface of the box. These flashed on and off with the flow of current through the densely packed electronic circuitry that filled the box. As the lights changed their pattern, flashing a spectrum of colors and shapes, a remarkable resemblance to a cartoonlike but oddly expressive human face could be seen.

It was Dr. Theopolis, one of the great computer brains of the Inner City. Physically helpless—for Dr. Theopolis and the other computer brains all possessed neither limbs nor implements, and had even to be carried around by a glittering metallic loop of chain links, like a twentieth-century woman's purse—the brains still carried out vital tasks for the citizens of the Inner City and for the city as a whole.

When they assembled in their meeting room, the computer brains collectively formed the high council of the Inner City. The theory upon which this council had been set up was as follows: any human administration has its limitations. If vested in a single person, the power of leadership inevitably leads to dictatorship and tyranny. If shared among various individuals and factions, the power tends to become divided and ineffective.

But by vesting the high decision-making powers of government in the greatest aggregation of electronic logic circuits and data-banks ever assembled, the Inner City was assured of government by completely objective intelligences, freed of the distractions of vanity and ambition, wishing only to serve the common good of the residents of the City and of all Earth. That was the plan: but so far, it had not been possible to separate out the emotions and be able to produce pure emotionless thought, even in the computer brains.

Soon after his first arrival at the Inner City, Buck Rogers had acquired both the robot Twiki and the computer brain Theopolis. The three had shared hair-raising adventures in savage Anarchia, in the Inner City, and in outer space itself.

Now Buck bent and lifted Theopolis. He examined the circuit-filled cube carefully. "I'm sorry, Dr. Theopolis. I didn't mean to sit on you. Are you all right?"

"I'm quite all right," the brain responded. Although lacking in extensible organs, the computer was fitted with audio sensors, video scanners, and a voder circuit—the computer equivalents of ears, eyes, and a voice.

"Yes, I'm all right," the computer repeated. "But I'll have you remember that I'm a highly sophisticated compuvisor, not a couch for the comfort of your inefficient protoplasmic embodiment."

"I'm sorry," Buck answered. "It was an accident. I got a shock trying to get Twiki back in shape."

"*Hmph!*" the computer brain exclaimed. "You have better ways to spend your time, don't you? Besides, you'll probably do more harm than good, messing around with the insides of a quad. Call Drone Repair."

"Right," Buck Rogers conceded. "Let my fingers do the walking."

"I beg your pardon?" the computer asked.

"Never mind." Buck picked up an intercom unit, one of the com-phones that connected every personal dwelling unit in Inner City with all of the city's support services. "Drone Repair, please." He waited a moment. Then, "Hi there. I've got this robot here, a quad model, designation Twiki. Darned thing threw a short."

There was a long silence on Buck's end while he listened.

Then Buck said, "Well, I can't compute either. I also can't fix the little mother. Wait a sec."

He held the phone out to Theopolis and asked him to try and get some service for Twiki.

"Drone Repair?" asked the computer's synthe-sized voice. "This is Theopolis one-four-eight-oh compuvisor. Report malfunction in Twiki drone five-three-two-slash-one-four-bee. Thank you." The computer's indicator lights flashed as if he were smiling up at Buck Rogers. To the spaceman he said, "You may replace the com-phone."

Buck replaced the phone, gave Theopolis and the unmoving Twiki a final glance, and headed for the door.

"Where are you going?" Theopolis called.

"Out," Buck said, distractedly.

"But you know you aren't permitted to leave the premises without clearing with me," Theopolis almost shouted.

"Well, I'm going to. What are you going to do about it?" Buck shot back.

"I'll have to report you," the computer declared solemnly.

"How?" Rogers asked, still standing in the door-way. "Twiki can't move until the short's repaired. You have no way to move around unless he carries you—which he can't—or I carry you—which I won't. You won't be able to file any reports till I get back, my friend."

Buck started to draw the door shut behind him. He still seemed distracted, with his mind miles away.

"But the Drone repairmen are coming here," Theopolis called after him.

Buck turned around and re-entered the room. "Good point," he muttered ruefully. "Guess I'll just have to take you with me. To keep you from squealing on me, as we used to say when I was a schoolkid in old Chi-town." His actions were as good as his words, as he reached for the computer brain and carefully placed its carrying-chain around his neck like a microphone cord.

"Where are we going?" Theopolis cried plaintively.

Buck Rogers ignored the question. He was staring at his feet, but he wasn't—apparently—thinking about his footwear. Buck stayed silent for long moments: then, at last, he snapped his head upright and started for the com-phone. "First," he said to Theopolis, who swung back and forth across Buck's chest as he walked, "I'll get Drone Repair on the horn again." He set Theopolis down on a table, and placed the com-phone unit next to the computer brain.

"Now," Buck said, "you relay info from those repair people, and we'll see if I can get Twiki back in working order using their info and my tools."

In twenty minutes Twiki's scanner lenses were flashing, his joints and limbs were mobile, and he uttered several short squeals.

Once more Buck placed Theopolis' carrying chain around his own neck; he stood up, and again he headed for the door.

"But where are we going?" Theopolis complained.

Buck didn't answer, just beckoned for Twiki to follow.

CHAPTER 4.

The Inner City of the twenty-fifth century stood like a last bastion of civilization against the encroaching night of savagery, barbarism, and death. Not that its leaders or its citizens saw their city in that light. On the contrary, they regarded themselves as the vanguard of a new blossoming for humankind, the most advanced center of learning and technology on a blighted planet, from where technicians who were almost missionaries of enlightenment went out to spread the influence of sanitation, organization, and rehabilitation over the burnt and poisoned Earth.

Still, between the ravages of barbarian tribes and the possible spread of plague through unpoliced contact between the Inner City and the denizens of Anarchia beyond, the leaders of the Inner City had seen fit to proclaim a strange sort of quarantine, a quarantine designed not to save a healthy world from a disease-bearing individual, but to protect an oasis of sanity and health from a world gone mad with sickness and hate.

The Inner City was walled like a castle keep of old, only its walls were of plastic and metal, of

force-fields and of electronic scanners rather than
of stone or wood.

The walls were guarded, and occasionally the
guards would turn their glances toward the city
they protected. But their concern was with keeping invaders out rather than citizens in, and little
attention was paid to the inside of the barriers.

As Buck Rogers crouched in the shadows of a
looming structure near the inner walls of the city,
he peered outward at the barrier and the personnel
staffing it. From the computer brain still hanging
at his neck rose a question: "Why are we at the
city wall?"

"Don't your batteries ever wear down?" Buck
whispered fiercely.

"What are batteries?" the computer asked.

"Be quiet or I'll break your nose," Buck answered logically.

"Hah! I don't have a—"

Buck muffled the end of the sentence by stuffing
a piece of soft cloth into the computer's speaker-
housing.

"—nose." Theopolis' last word was hardly audi-
ble.

With the computer hanging from his neck, Buck
sprinted to a public intercom station, with Twiki
right behind him. Buck grabbed the intercom
speaker and gasped into it, in the voice of a near-
panicked man, "Wall security. Fast!" There was a
pause. Then Buck said, "Hello. I see some sus-
picious-looking characters lurking around Entrance
11. You'd better get someone here fast. I think
they look like Draconians."

As com-central flashed word back to the wall,

the guards at Entrances 10 and 12 dashed toward
Entrance 11, ready to intercept the intruders and
take them into custody.

As soon as the entrances were cleared Buck
Rogers leaped into a public-transit landcar. These
vehicles were part of the municipal service offered
by the Inner City: by stationing a sufficient number of them around its territory for the free use of
citizens beyond the range of the streamlined monorail system, far less equipment and fuel was committed than had been the case in the days of
private automobiles when billions upon billions of
dollars were tied up in the maintenance of millions
of vehicles that stood idle most of the time.

The Inner City landcar was a sleek, low-slung
vehicle that skimmed along the smooth roadways
and special tracks of the Inner City quietly, rapidly,
and safely.

But Buck Rogers pressed the manual override
button that disconnected the landcar's automatic
guidance system and turned it from a part of the
city's arterial flow, transformed it to an independent vehicle. Buck, with Twiki seated beside
him, pointed it squarely at Entrance 11, ran up
the power to its peak level, and zoomed out of the
Inner City, into the dangerous and ill-explored
regions vaguely designated as Anarchia.

Here, beyond the city walls, all was loneliness
and desolation. A weird moon shone down on the
Earth. Unlike the white or silvery-yellow light of
the ancient moon, the satellite of Earth's twenty-
fifth century cast a baleful reddish glow across
the poisoned surface of the planet.

Strange shadows leaped and shrank in the

blood-red moonlight. Equally strange sounds were carried by night winds—sounds of animals and soughings of trees, boomings as of distant surf, as if ancient Lake Michigan had become a huge inland sea, and vague noises that might have been made by manlike beasts or beastlike men somewhere in the dark.

Theopolis tried futilely to speak through the clogged speaker of his box. Buck Rogers reached into the speaker-enclosure and removed the impromptu gag. "What is it?" the spaceman demanded in a soft voice. "And be quiet or I'll jump up and down on you."

Theopolis took the warning. "I said, where are we?"

"Anarchia."

"You are not allowed in Anarchia, Captain Rogers. It's dangerous."

"Huh!" Buck grunted. "You call this dangerous? You should have seen this city when I was a kid. Chicago—or Detroit—or New York! Now, *they* were dangerous!"

Theopolis fell silent. Twiki was silent, but his scanner lenses flashed up and down, back and forth.

Buck, too, scanned the scene, from where they stood out to the horizon. In the distance he could make out a campfire of sorts. Mutants were standing and sitting around it, trying to keep warm in the chilly night air near what had once been Lake Michigan. Ancient ruins surrounded the campfire.

Buck propelled the landcar forward. As he drew nearer to the encampment a pile of rubble, disturbed by some force-effect emanating from the groundcar, tumbled across the pathway. Buck swung the landcar desperately away from the tumbling debris, found the car headed toward an even worse obstacle, hit the brake sharply and swung back barely in time to avoid a crash, but as he did so the vehicle's engine coughed and fell silent.

Buck struggled with the unfamiliar controls, trying to restart the futuristic vehicle.

As he did so, the mutants clustered around the campfire began to advance toward the landcar.

Buck flipped the main power control of the landcar, hit the automatic starting control, fed power to the vehicle's mechanism.

The mutants advanced, growing more confident as the landcar failed to respond.

Finally the landcar returned to life, but by now it was completely surrounded by hulking, menacing figures, the red light of the distant campfire and the baleful moon reflecting like gore from their bleary eyes.

They circled the landcar, reaching tentatively to pat and feel its surface, then reaching more boldly toward Buck or Theopolis or Twiki. They spoke no language recognizable as such, but grunted and mumbled a patois of half-articulate noises more akin to the mouthings of animals than the speech of men.

Buck tried slowly to back the landcar away from the mutants, but they had surrounded it entirely by now. He wasn't ready to ram them and run them down—perhaps later he might wish that he had, but for now he still regarded them as humans, however degraded, and he couldn't bring himself to crash into them coldbloodedly.

Instead he tried a contrived expression of friendly cheer; he spoke in hopes that they might understand his tone of voice if not his words: "Uh—hi." Buck ventured, "You, uh, guys got a really nice place here, don't you?"

He attempted again to edge the landcar through their ranks without maiming or killing any of the threatening mutants. "Uh, hate to eat and run like this."

He tried once more to back the landcar away from the others, but only succeeded in moving it a short distance.

"Uh, listen, if you're ever in the neighborhood, look me up."

He backed the car a bit more, but the mutants began to cluster behind the vehicle, clearly beginning to understand Buck's attempt to ease his way through the thinnest portion of their ranks.

"Maybe you'd like some silk stockings? Chocolate bars?" The mutants continued to gather in the rearward path of the landcar, ignoring Buck's distracting banter. "Would ya?" he tried again. "No? Huh, guess not."

By now almost all of the mutants had clustered behind the landcar. "Well, that's okay," Buck told the mutants, "'cause I don't have any anyway. Heh-heh," he laughed nervously. Twiki squealed.

The mutants were now concentrated at the rear of the car. As if at some unseen and unheard signal, they launched themselves toward the car in a murderous, concerted rush.

Simultaneously with the move of the half-men,

Buck slammed the landcar from reverse into forward gear. The car lurched forward. Buck shouted
an ancient battle cry. The vehicle slammed into
the debris of centuries.

It was a desperate risk. If the debris had slagged
into a solid mass with the passing decades and
centuries, there was no way that the landcar—or
its occupants!—could possibly survive the impact.
But if the debris had instead undergone a sort of
dry rot, slowly disintegrating into a weakened
mass of material with the alternate expansion and
contraction, soaking and evaporation of rain and
snow for the past five hundred years—then the
landcar could plow through it like a motorcyclist
sloughing through a mountain of shaving cream.

There was a terrific sense of impact and a sound
like a *whumpf!*—and then the landcar was through
the debris. Shards and fragments of accumulated
junk cascaded through the air behind the landcar.
The mutants, outwitted and outmaneuvered,
shouted their frustration and defiance, shaking
fists and futilely hurling missiles after the landcar.

Safely beyond the mutant encampment, Buck
pulled the landcar to a halt. Its formerly smooth
and handsome surface was now crumpled and
covered with muck and fragments of debris, but
its engine continued to run. Buck slumped in his
seat, catching his breath and regaining his composure from the nearly fatal encounter with the
mutant band.

Theopolis took advantage of the momentary
calm to plead once more with the spaceman. "You
should go back," the computer brain initiated his

THAT MAN ON BETA

appeal, and Twiki emitted a series of clicks and
one squeal while the computer brain's voder spoke.

"I can't," Buck snapped back before the machines could go on. "I've got to track down my
family."

"You won't find out anything," Theopolis
argued. The lights behind his plexiglass covering
flashed dismally. "Give up and go back, Rogers.
You barely escaped with your life. Next time you
might not be so lucky."

"That wasn't luck," Buck cracked in reply, "it
was skill, intellect, and pure animal magnetism."

"*And* a lot of luck," Theopolis insisted.

But the exchange was over. The computer had
made his appeal, the spaceman had rejected it,
and now Buck set the landcar to rolling forward
once again, rolling cautiously but steadily through
the rubble-littered streets of Anarchia, the dismal
hell that once had been Chicago.

In the distance Buck could hear the waves of
Lake Michigan hissing and crashing against the
shore. The Chicago River bridges had all fallen
long ago, but Buck managed to find a sort of
accidental bridge formed by the crash of the
ancient IBM Building, which threw a dam of
rubble across the river. The water had made its
way through the cracks and submerged gaps in
the debris, so pressure had never built up and
swept away the dam, and Buck was able to pick
his way across the runneled surface, the dark, oily
waters of the poisoned river to either side of the
landcar.

"Oh, be careful, will you, Buck," Theopolis
pleaded.

The drone Twiki squealed.

"Yes, Twiki, of course Buck is a good driver," Theopolis soothed. "I'm sure he won't dump us into the river."

Again the drone gave its characteristic, high-pitched sound.

"Yes," Theopolis told the drone. "I'm sure that Buck understands that we'd sink. Why, if we were to rust away there beneath the water he'd lose the two best friends he has in the world. Now, just be calm and we'll be on the other side in a few seconds."

The landcar rolled from the impromptu dam onto the ground on the other side of the Chicago River. Buck breathed a sigh of relief. "Theopolis," he said, "do you really understand those clunks and squeals that Twiki makes, or is that all some sort of put-on for my benefit?"

"Why, Buck!" the computer's lights glowed indignantly. "How could you even accuse me of falsifying data in that fashion? It would blow half the capacitors in my monitor to do such a thing!"

Buck drove through an open area that might once have been a grassy municipal park. He brought the landcar as close as he could to the remnants of an immense structure, then turned off its engine. "If I haven't forgotten the layout of this burg in the past five centuries, this is City Hall. I've got some checking to do inside, and I don't want to leave the landcar unguarded. Do you think you can handle the job, Theopolis? Twiki?"

The drone made a terrified-sounding squeal and began to rock from side to side in its seat.

"Now stop that!" Theopolis ordered.

Twiki calmed down—a little.

"Of course we can, Buck," the computer said. "You go attend to your business, and we'll be here in the landcar when you get back. We don't get bored, you know—I can always fill the time by calculating the lunar ephemeris for arbitrarily selected periods a few billion years from now. You never know when that information is going to come in handy."

CHAPTER 5.

The once-imposing great doors of City Hall had long since fallen in on their hinges, leaving easy access to the main vestibule of the building. Here Buck found a larger-than-life, awesome pedestal marked with the name Richard Daley, and the feet of a statue still on the pedestal. Buck looked above the metal feet, visualizing as best he could the invisible man who stood smiling benevolently at long-dead voters.

As he stood contemplating the ruined monument he became aware of a sound—the sound of breathing, suppressed, shallow, nearly inaudible. Nearly: but not quite.

He cocked his head, zeroed in on the source of the sound, yanked a shard of fallen wainscotting away from its place and saw—an impromptu shelter holding two children in tattered rags. There were a boy and a girl. They stared up at Buck in abject terror, making no attempt to escape or to attack. They merely crouched, trembling, awaiting his reaction to them.

"I won't hurt you," Buck said to the children.

There was no response.

"Can't you talk?" Buck asked.

"I can talk," the girl said at length. She pointed to the boy. "He can't talk. I can."

Buck looked at the boy crouching mutely beside the girl.

"He your brother?" the spaceman asked.

The girl pondered. "Maybe. Who are you?"

"I'm from the Inner City," Buck said.

The statement brought an unexpected reaction. The girl's eyes widened in terror. Without a word she bolted from her hiding place, dodged past Buck's surprised arms and bolted across the vestibule.

Buck took off in hot pursuit.

The girl headed up a flight of broad marble stairs heavily choked with fallen debris.

Buck lunged, caught her by one filthy, naked ankle. She struggled until it was clear that Buck had no intention of letting go and she had no chance of breaking his grip. Then the girl subsided into resigned passivity.

"I said I won't hurt you," Buck told the girl again. "Why are you so afraid of the Inner City?"

"I'm not afraid," the girl exclaimed defiantly, "I'm not afraid of anything!"

The silent boy emerged from his hiding place and timidly approached Buck and the girl. He was unarmed and apparently harmless. Buck decided to permit him to stand by while he interrogated the girl.

"Do you live here?"

"Yes," the girl conceded. "This is our home."

Buck looked earnestly into the girl's face. "Now this is very important. Please. Do you know where the Hall of Records is? A huge room full of files, birth certificates, things like that? You know, just mountains of paper."

"Oh yes. Sure, a big room full of papers. I'll show you."

The two children led Buck up the flight of marble stairs, down a dark hallway choked with the dust and trash of five centuries. The spaceman jumped when a huge shadowy shape appeared, then ran silently across their path: a gigantic rat. The children took the event as a matter of course and continued to lead Buck along the hallway, through broken doors.

They stopped where a cable ran through a hole in the ceiling. The girl first, then the boy, jumped from their feet, caught the cable and began to shimmy up it as confidently and easily as two monkeys climbing a liana-vine in some tropical jungle.

Buck grasped the cable, preparatory to lifting himself after the children. "Are you sure this is the best way?" he called up to them. "How about the stairs?"

"The stairs are sealed off," the girl called back down to him. "This is the only way."

The cable brought them into another echoing, dusty chamber. Buck followed the children along another corridor, wondering momentarily if he was being led into an ambush. But at that moment there opened before him the prospect he had been seeking: one of the largest rooms he had ever beheld. It was nearly as large as the launching bay of the now defunct starship *Draconia*, as large as a starfighter hangar at the Inner City spaceport, as large as the old Vehicle Assembly Building at old Cape Canaveral, back during Buck's first life-time in the twentieth century.

And it was filled with a five-hundred-year-old shambles.

Uncountable metal filing cabinets stood about, lay on the floor, hung at precarious angles. Some were open, some rusted shut, some still obviously full, others with their contents strewn wildly across the dust-laden marble floor.

Buck stumbled around the room, stunned by the experience. He stopped, lifted a crumbling document, tossed it aside and seized another. "My God," he muttered, "it looks like . . . a holocaust."

"It was," the girl agreed. "This is the heritage of the great holocaust."

"What happened?" Buck asked.

"I don't know," the girl shook her head. Through the caked dust and straggly curls, she managed somehow to have the beauty of child-hood's innocence. "The holocaust was hundreds of years ago," she went on. "We know that there was a terrible destruction and plague visited upon us—or our ancestors. But no one is old enough to remember what happened, and the tales we are told do not tell either."

Buck smiled grimly. "Some of us are *too* old to remember," he said, more to himself than to the child. "Well"—he picked up another file, then cast it aside—"there's nothing here newer than 1988. There's nothing here that can help me."

Suddenly a mellow, yet oddly mechanical voice was heard. "I told you you'd find nothing."

The girl jumped, startled.

Buck whirled and saw the robot Twiki with Dr.

Theopolis suspended around his metallic neck.
"What are you doing here?" Buck demanded. "I
thought you were guarding the car."

"There's no one out there, no danger, Buck. I
decided that you might need my wise counsel in
your researches, so I asked Twiki here to bring
me in."

The robot squeaked—several short, annoyed-
sounding squeaks.

"Oh, all right," Theopolis said. "Yes, it is kind
of spooky out there and we both feel better being
with Captain Rogers."

The young girl interrupted the exchange. "What
is that thing?" she asked, pointing to Twiki and
Theopolis, apparently mistaking them for a single
device.

"It's a pain in the diode," Buck said. He cast a
last, despairing look at the scattered files of the
hall, then turned and began to make his way back
toward the ground floor and the street. In a few
minutes he and the robot-team were climbing
back into their groundcar. Buck turned and smiled
at the two children. "I'd like to pay you for the
help you gave me," he said. He reached into his
pocket and pulled out a quantity of Inner City
scrip.

"What's that?" the girl asked.

"Money."

"Never heard of it. What's it for?"

Buck shoved the scrip back in his pocket and
pulled off his coat, aware that both children were
trembling in the chilly air. "Here, try this," he
held the coat toward the girl.

She tried it on, petted it, ducked her head and murmured, "Thank you," to Buck. Her brother came up and rubbed his face on the cloth of the sleeve. The girl pulled off the coat and slipped it around her brother's shoulders. It fit him like a circus tent. "There," the girl said, "he needs it more, he's colder than I am. And it fits him better, anyhow. Where are you going?" she asked Buck suddenly.

"I don't know," he confessed. "I'm trying to find some information. I'd hoped to find it in the Hall of Records. But. . ." He shrugged helplessly.

"Maybe Pandro can help you," the girl said. "He was here yesterday."

"Who's Pandro?"

"Boss of the gypsies."

"Gypsies!" Buck exclaimed. "There are still gypsies?"

"Oh, sure. They come through every so often. They're camped pretty near here now."

Buck's landcar approached the gypsy encampment through the gloom that seemed to hover perpetually in Anarchia, be it day or night, summer or winter. The encampment, to Buck's first glimpse, resembled a bizarre parody of the traditional gypsy encampment. Campfires burned in a roughly circular clearing while colorfully dressed men and women circulated, chattering and visiting one another; pots of food hung, bubbling and smoking, over fires—that much was just as usual. The gypsy vehicles were drawn up around the clearing, but instead of the horse-drawn wagons

of wood and canvas that Buck in his boyhood had
associated with gypsies, these were a fleet of camp-
ers, motor homes, and recreational vehicles. They
were dusty and rust-marred, battered, painted and
repainted beyond any hope of ever determining
their original shape and color. But as Buck approached he saw a gypsy arriving on a rusty, fend-
erless motorcycle—so somehow the gypsies
managed to keep their power-packs replenished
and their running gear functional, at least on one
heavy, German-made motorcycle.

Buck climbed from the landcar. He reached
toward Twiki and lifted Dr. Theopolis from
around the drone's neck. "I may need some of
that wise counsel you were peddling, Theopolis.
Twiki, stay here. Stay out of trouble if you can.
I'll be back." With a careful movement, Buck
hung the computer brain around his own neck.

Twiki squealed in angry protest but obeyed,
remaining in the landcar as Buck walked into the
gypsy encampment. He walked slowly up to a
woman in almost traditional gypsy garb and offered a tentative greeting.

"Howdy, howdy!" the woman responded.
"What's your handle?"

Buck looked around helplessly, finally asked,
"Uh . . . can you tell me where I can find Pandro?"

"Over your shoulder. Come on," the woman said.

Buck gaped at her but she didn't move. He
turned his head and looked over his shoulder. All
he could see was a half-demolished recreational
vehicle.

"Pandro," Buck tried again. Maybe the woman

mistook his meaning. "*Pan-dro*," he repeated, "do you understand me?"

"Wall to wall and treetop tall," the woman said. "Don't you have no ears?"

Buck wondered what the woman meant, whether she understood him. She *seemed* to speak English. Her words were ordinary enough, and her sentences were gramatically correct. But they didn't *mean* anything! He smiled, walked to the half-demolished cruiser. He pounded on the door and asked, "Pandro? You in there?"

"Bright-eyed and bushy-tailed," a voice called back. The vehicle's door opened. A man gazed out at Buck. The man was middle-aged, a grizzled-looking, stubble-faced, tough- and competent-looking man who had clearly done his share of rough living, survived it, and emerged battered but unbowed.

Buck introduced himself.

"It's your nickel," the grizzled man said.

"Uh-huh." Buck stood looking up at the other man. "Can I come in?"

"You got the break," the man said. "I'll pour coffee on ya." He gestured Buck into the vehicle, offered him a seat, poured him a cup of some vile greenish stuff that he claimed was coffee.

Buck made a face at the vicious brew. Well, at least it was hot, whatever other shortcomings it might suffer from. Buck explained his mission, finished with a request. "Anything. Any clues, leads to my family. What happened to them? Do any of my descendants still survive?"

"I don't know nothing," Pandro answered. "But

I know a good buddy that might could help ya. Handle's Aris. Very old dude, been breathin' longer as anybody I know. And he's got smarts he ain't even used yet. Lives in Skipland."

"Great. Skipland, eh? How do I find him?"

"I need some greenstamps," Pandro stated.

"Greenstamps?" Buck saw Pandro make a gesture. "Oh, sure. He reached into his pocket again, pulled out the same Inner City scrip that he'd previously offered to the girl at the Hall of Records. "How much?" he asked.

"That ain't greenstamps," Pandro said. "Not in this lane."

"Then what's greenstamps?" Buck asked.

"Could be most anything. I can't use it, I'll trade it off." He pointed to Buck's laser-gun. "Like that smokey stunner, f'rinstance."

"You mean my laser?"

"Pository."

Before Buck could reply to the demand, Theopolis put in, "Giving him a weapon is forbidden, Captain Rogers."

At the sound of the strange voice, Pandro jumped. He stared wildly around, looking for the source of the words.

"It's all right," Buck explained. "There's no one else here. It was this box that I'm wearing. It talks."

Pandro bent and stared at Theopolis, almost hypnotized by the arrays of flashing lights within the plexiglass. "Come again?"

"Theopolis," Buck commanded, "say something. Pandro wants to hear you talk."

The computer remained silent.

"Dr. Theopolis, I'm warning you," Buck fumed. "Talk!"

Nothing.

"He's being quiet just to make me mad," Buck explained thinly. "I kept telling him to shut up, earlier. Now he's sulking. Talk, Theo!"

"Ah, you're pulling my antenna," Pandro laughed. "That thing don't talk. But I like them lights, them's real pretty. I know a chick who'd fancy that box for a decoration. So you give me it and I'll Q.S.O. ya Aris' 10-20."

"Does that mean you'll tell me how to find him?" Buck asked.

Pandro nodded, still staring at Theopolis' lights. "Four ten."

"Okay," Buck said. "It's a deal." He removed the computer's strap from his neck and handed the plexiglass box to Pandro.

"No," Theopolis shrieked. "You can't do that!"

"Hey!" Pandro exclaimed, almost dropping the box. "It really talked!"

"And now it's your turn, good buddy," Buck answered.

"Way off in Skipland where the big cliffs have faces," Pandro said. "Just under the faces is a cave. That's Aris' home 20."

"How far?" Buck asked. "Which way?"

Pandro pointed outside the vehicle. "That way," he said. "'Bout half a day's ride if you drop your hammer in that roller skate of yours."

Buck frowned with concentration. "Mount Rushmore?"

"A big ten-four," Pandro grinned.

Buck offered his thanks, started toward Pandro's

door, then turned back for a moment. "Tell me, Pandro, why do you people talk that way?"

Pandro looked blank. "What way?"

Buck shook his head. "Never mind." He climbed from the vehicle, stood outside. "So long," he added, starting toward his landcar.

"Threes on ya," Pandro called after Buck. As soon as the spaceman had pulled away in his landcar, Pandro turned back toward Dr. Theopolis. "Talking box, huh?" the gypsy gritted. "Otherwise known as compuvisor model Theo 1480, member of the Inner City council. But a dumb old buddy like me wouldn't know that, would I?"

He grinned, opened a section of wall inside his camper, entered a glittering, ultramodern communications room. He stepped inside, pressed a series of controls and spoke into a microphone. "Pandro here, looking for a break. Excelsior. Come on."

The answer that came seemed to carry an almost tangible air of remoteness and bitter cold. "This is Excelsior," the voice said. "Go ahead, Pandro." The voice called itself Excelsior, but to those who could identify its owner it was clear who the voice of Excelsior really belonged to: Kane. "Have you located Rogers, Pandro?"

"Located?" the gypsy leader replied. "You bet! He fell right on my head. Just like we planned."

The cold voice gave an oily chuckle. "You sent him to see Aris, Pandro?"

"Rodger-dodger. And I copped his compuvisor into the bargain!"

"Oh, wonderful, Pandro," Kane gloated. "Wonderful! Oh, ho-ho-ho-ho-ho! The Gregorians had better beware!"

"A big ten-four, good Draconian buddy." Pandro switched off his transmitter.

CHAPTER 6.

Colonel Wilma Deering was walking across the tarmac at Inner City spaceport, en route from her office to the armaments hangar. This was no matter of critical urgency, no exciting new development: it was part of her daily routine, part of the never-ending responsibility of command.

She was surprised by a gentle touch at her elbow, turned, exclaimed, "Dr. Huer! What are you doing out here at the spaceport?"

"Just a little informal call," the aged scientist explained. The bright daylight gleamed off his old-fashioned spectacles as he looked up into Wilma's face. "I'm a little worried about Captain Rogers, Colonel. Perhaps you've been working him too hard. The sensor readouts turned up an alert on him the other morning."

Wilma shrugged. "Nothing unusual in that. Could be anything. Maybe he was up celebrating something the night before. He couldn't make it to my fancy Clipsop dinner!"

"No, my dear, it wasn't just that. In fact, we had alerts on Captain Rogers three mornings running. His overall metab ratings have dropped 12 leers.

But we couldn't find any physiological cause in the sensor readouts!"

"Then it must be psychological, obviously. You know, I am concerned for the health and welfare of my command, Dr. Huer. But I've always had my reservations about Rogers—his emotional stability, his psychological suitability for his assignment. A man from five hundred years in the past is going to have problems adjusting, no matter how well he seems outwardly to fit in."

"Suppose he'd been staying up all night, Wilma? Night after night. That would explain the metab drop, wouldn't it?"

Wilma halted and faced Dr. Huer. "Captain Rogers' ship is right over there," she gestured. "Let's see if he's in it. Most of our pilots spend a lot of hours working over their ships. The ground crews that we have are tops, you know—but it's the pilots who put their lives on the line every time they fly."

They peered into Buck's ship, saw a figure stretched across the cockpit. For a moment he appeared to be dead, but a slow, steady rise and fall of his chest showed that he was merely napping.

"There you are, Doctor," Wilma said. "I just think he's been working by day and playing by night, and it's finally caught up with him. And I'm going to find out what's going on!"

Just hours later, Buck and Wilma threaded their way through the crush of close-set tables in the Palace of Mirrors lounge in the Inner City. The lounge was the smartest watering-hole in this twenty-fifth century capital. Men in neatly cut outfits and women in dazzling, daring gowns drank, dined, chatted, table-hopped, gazed at the spectacular light-and-water show on the stage or danced to the weirdly beautiful and compelling electronic music of a robot symphonium that occupied the center of the room.

To Buck the scene was not wholly unfamiliar. Some of the more fashionable nightclubs of his own twentieth century had been not unlike the Palace of Mirrors lounge. Still, the strange music, modernistic decor, and general sense of displacement and alienation that seemed to dog his feet bothered him more than usual in this place.

"Here," Wilma announced as she spotted a vacant table. "Told you I'd find us one. I still don't understand your twentieth-century custom of tipping headwaiters to get you tables. It sounds like bribery to me."

They sat down and Buck surveyed the teeming room. "Nice place they've got here. Too bad they can't get any customers."

"Buck," Wilma said happily, "I'm glad we could get away from the spacefield and the defense squadron. Not that I hate my job. I can hardly think of one I'd swap it for. But a change is good now and then."

Buck smiled at her across the table. "Right you are." He looked up at the approach of a diminutive, vaguely humanoid figure. It was a drone, somewhat similar to Twiki but equipped with the implements needed by a waiter. Its formal outfit seemed to be enameled onto its metal body, and its discreet lapel nametag read simply R-8.

"May I have your order, please?" the drone asked Buck and Wilma. There was a permanent ingratiating smile on its face.

Chuckling at the ludicrous drone, Buck asked, "Did you ever have a job as a clown?"

The drone stood buzzing for a few seconds, then recycled through its command loop. "May I have your order, please?"

"Hey," Buck exclaimed, "that reminds me. I haven't had a Big Mac in about five hundred years. Hey, R-8, what's the chances of getting a Big Mac around this joint?" And Buck began to laugh loudly, inexplicably.

The waiter buzzed some more and repeated its standard query.

"Buck," Wilma interrupted the odd dialogue, "what's a Big Mac?"

"That's the funny part," Buck replied, wiping the tears of laughter from his eyes. "We didn't know what it was back in the old days either. We just swallowed it and hoped for the best."

Wilma turned toward the drone. "We'll have two servings of protein 4-S and Vinol, please."

The quad bowed ludicrously, thanked Wilma and tottered away through the narrow, crowded spaces between diners' tables.

As soon as the drone had departed, Buck looked at Wilma more seriously. "I'm sorry I got so carried away, Wilma. I was almost hysterical, wasn't I?"

She didn't speak, but Buck could see the answer in her serious expression.

"I think I'm just exhausted," Buck resumed. I haven't been getting much sleep, and. . ."

"I know, Buck. That's what I wanted to talk to you about," Wilma put in. "I know what you've been doing."

He showed his surprise. "You do?"

Wilma nodded slowly. "Yes. And I want you to know that it's all right with me. Our official relationship is a separate matter, of course. But on a personal level, I know I have no hold on you. No strings. And—Buck—we can still be friends, I hope."

"Hey," the spaceman replied, "I'm really relieved about that. I thought you'd be mad at me. Sure, I want to be friends."

"Good," Wilma smiled wistfully. Her smile started to waver and threatened to turn into tears. She turned her face away.

"Wilma." Buck reached to take her hand but she pulled it away. "Wilma, what's the matter?"

The drone-waiter tottered back to their table and placed a bottle of Vinol and two glasses on the table. Then it tottered away again. Buck, waiting for Wilma to regain her composure, reached for the Vinol and poured each of them a glass.

Wilma took a deep breath and faced Buck again. "There's nothing the matter, Buck. I wish you the very best. I only wish that you'd—you'd told me about it instead of being so sneaky. That's all."

"Well," Buck frowned, "I *couldn't* tell you. Dr. Huer denied me permission. If I'd told you, you would have had a duty to try to stop me. We were through that all before, we'd have been back to square one."

"Why would Dr. Huer do that?" Wilma asked. She watched Buck raise his glass and sip at the Vinol. "Why would you need anybody's permission, for that matter? Sex is a personal matter in the Inner City."

Now it was Buck's turn to be nonplussed. In fact, he half-choked on the Vinol he was sipping. Wilma and R-8 both had to pound him on the back to clear his windpipe of the Vinol. "Thanks, thanks," Buck gasped. "Uh—Wilma. Wilma, eh, what do you mean by sex?"

The beautiful starfighter commander blushed, her skin glowing from the roots of her softly curved hair to the very low neckline of her daringly cut formal gown. "Buck, I know that a lot of things have changed in the five hundred years since your era. But some things have stayed the same, I'm sure. I know that you've been out all night, every night, lately. I assume that you've been seeing someone. Isn't that logical?"

"Oh!" Buck exclaimed. "Oh, sure! Of course, Wilma," he said, stalling a little till he could think of what to say. "Well, I didn't want to upset you, you see."

"Yes, I see. Thank you for your thoughtfulness, Buck." She paused, then asked, "Is she anyone I know, Buck?"

Before Buck could answer the R-8 returned with their protein. It was a tiny platter of hard nuggets looking something like irregularly shaped ball bearings or gravel. Buck looked distastefully at the dish of food. "Thanks a lot," he told the waiter as it tottered away. Then, to Wilma, he said, "Look at this funny food, will ya? I'm still not used to this stuff."

"It's very filling," Wilma Deering said dully. "It swells in your stomach."

Buck picked up a piece of the protein, turned it around and around, examining it from all angles. "Too bad it couldn't swell in the kitchen," he commented. He popped the pebblelike bit of nourishment into his mouth. "Mmm, I can almost taste it."

"Buck, why won't you tell me about her?" Wilma brought the subject back to its former focus.

"Terrific light show, isn't it?" the spaceman asked. "I sure hope that water-act doesn't get loose and drench all these wonderful munchies!"

"All right," Wilma conceded. "It's none of my business, is that it?"

"No," Buck shook his head, "it isn't that at all. Please don't feel that way, Wilma. I do care for your feelings. And—she's a terrific girl. I know you'd really like her. Lots. Her name is—" He hesitated, then resumed. "—Lisa. She has very fair skin, and she's built like, well, she's sort of on the thin side."

"I see," Wilma murmured.

"But, boy," Buck added softly, "can she ever type!"

Wilma's expression—one of barely contained heartbreak—began to change slowly to one of puzzlement and suspicion. "Buck," she said, "in our society, women don't type. Robots do."

"Oh," Buck exclaimed—as though he were startled, or alarmed—"so that's why her feet get so cold in the middle of the night!"

The next day, Wilma sat opposite Dr. Huer in his sparkling, efficient, glowing white office. "And then," the defense squadron commander was saying, "and then—then he described a *robot*!"

"Good heavens," Huer exploded, "didn't he even know the difference? My Lisa 5 is pretty realistic, but one would expect a grown man to be able to . . . or maybe he *does* know the difference and he prefers a robot to a human being! There have been cases in the past, you know. Severe alienation, fetishism, and so on. This can be a very serious matter. Perhaps I should have a talk with Captain Rogers."

"It won't do you any good, Dr. Huer, he won't tell you a thing. But I'm going to find out for myself what he's up to!"

Within the hour she was at Buck Rogers' personal dwelling facility—what he would have called, in twentieth-century Chicago, a one-room apartment. Wilma glanced carefully through a slitted opening, then edged into the room as quietly as she could.

She examined the room carefully to make sure that Buck was absent, then began a careful examination of the contents of the room—Buck's clothing, his personal belongings, toilet articles, spare military uniforms. The robot Twiki was there, unmoving, with its lights all out. Wilma remembered Buck's saying his own repairs to Twiki had finally been inadequate, and he was waiting for Drone Repair to take the robot into their shop for a thorough cleaning and a thorough checking of the circuitry.

Finally satisfied—or satisfied, at least, that there was nothing of interest to be found, she spoke: "Theo?"

"Theo?"

There was no answer.

"Theopolis? Dr. Theopolis?"

Still no response.

Puzzled, Wilma renewed her search of the room, calling out from time to time, "Dr. Theopolis, where are you?"

But there was no answer from Dr. Theopolis— he was elsewhere; and if Wilma Deering was mildly puzzled and distraught at her inability to locate the computer brain, that was nothing compared to the emotional state in which Dr. Theopolis was himself.

"I demand that you return me to Earth at once!" Theopolis exclaimed. "You have no right to bring me here!" If the computer's carefully synthesized voice, mild and reassuring, had been capable of an outraged screech, that would have been the term best applied to the tone in which he expressed himself.

In fact, mild and reassuring or not, Theopolis managed to deliver an outraged screech, something very close to a scream of rage: *This is an act of war!*

But for all that the computer brain was carried away into a near-hysterical state by his reactions to the situation in which he found himself, the men who handled him felt and showed nothing but glee at the machine's obvious discomfiture.

The first of these men was a Draconian space

pilot, who wearily undogged the hatch of his rocket ship and climbed gratefully from the craft. It was the end of the long flight from Earth to Villus Beta, and the pilot was sweat-soaked and muscle-weary. But the pilot was not too exhausted to smile smugly as he handed Dr. Theopolis to the burly, greasy-visaged figure who was waiting for the delivery of the rectangle of angrily flashing light panels.

"An act of war, you say?" Kane echoed the enraged Theopolis. "An act of war, eh? Why, how very perceptive of you, you sweet little bundle of wires and tubes."

"Wires?" Theopolis screeched. "Tubes?" He flashed through a spectrum of orange, purple, and red shades. "I'll have you know that I'm built of the most modern components—fiber-optic cables, micro-miniaturized photo-etched supersilicon circuit modules, micromolecular array processors! There's not a blessed wire or tube in my body! Hasn't been one in my family for generations!"

Kane planted his feet wide apart, held the outraged Theopolis before him with one hand while he jammed his other fist onto a beefy hip, and roared with laughter.

And all the while that poor Theopolis, forwarded by the double-dealing Pandro to the oily Kane on Villus Beta, shrieked impotently at his mistreatment, Wilma Deering was still keeping watch at Captain William "Buck" Rogers' quarters. She had left the little room well before dark descended on the Inner City, and stationed herself so she could see his every coming and going.

The lights were on in Buck's quarters, and he

was carefully decking himself out in a fresh set of civilian clothing for the evening. Wilma saw him switch off the lights and close the door of his room—behind himself.

Before the spaceman could emerge from the building that contained his individual dwelling facility, Wilma flicked a jimmy into the lock on his landcar—or the landcar that he had arrived in and left standing outside his quarters, at any rate. She climbed into the vehicle, secreted herself in its luggage carrier, and waited impatiently until Buck emerged from the building, opened the car door, and climbed in.

Wilma didn't know whether Buck's story of a love affair with a robot was the truth or a fairy tale, but she was going to find out! The car moved along, its power-pack-energized engine purring smoothly. Wilma assumed that the trip would be for a few minutes, to some other location in this section of the Inner City, for if Buck was keeping a rendezvous on the other side of the dome he would simply have taken the monorail and switched to a groundcar at the other end.

But the car moved along for minutes, then for what seemed like hours. Wilma became puzzled. Was Buck driving to the far edge of the dome for some reason? And—the car *still* went on. Suddenly a chilling thought gripped Wilma's mind: maybe Buck *wasn't* keeping a rendezvous in the Inner City. Maybe he was defying both defense squadron discipline and Dr. Huer's specific ban on leaving the dome except in the line of duty.

Maybe he was heading into Anarchia!

Lulled by the steady purring of the landcar's

engine and the throbbing, almost purring vibration of the vehicle, Wilma found herself growing drowsy. She slept, dreamed disquieting dreams of Buck Rogers cavorting romantically with a slim, pale, beautiful rival of Wilma's, who turned into a clanking, deadly machine and made off with the spaceman while Wilma wept impotently.

She awakened with a jolt.

The car had halted, its engine had ceased to purr. Wilma could hear Buck open the landcar's door and climb out. She waited a few seconds and followed him.

As she emerged from the landcar she stood awestruck, staring at the sight above.

The night was unusually clear for the Earth of the twenty-fifth century. The moon was full and its red glow illuminated all of the landscape around the car. Towering above Wilma was the most astonishing sight she had ever beheld: four great faces stared stonily straight ahead. Each was as tall as a fast, single-seater rocket ship. They looked as natural as if they were living creatures just emerging from the Earth, their skins painted in almost healthy tones by the ruddy glare of the full moon. They had been carved from the rock— and Wilma suppressed a gasp. It seemed to her that the stunning faces were alive, that the rock they grew from was somehow living rock.

As soon as she had regained her composure she looked around.

There he was! Buck Rogers was advancing across the open ground toward the great carven faces. Wilma dodged behind boulders and shrubbery each time Buck stopped to survey the ground.

He climbed up the final steep approach to the statues.

Wilma gasped as she saw Buck disappear into the rock!

Could he have obtained some scientific device that made it possible for a man to walk through rock? Wilma ran the last few yards to the point where Buck had disappeared. No, he hadn't penetrated the solid rock. There was a cave here!

Inside, Buck Rogers shone a pocket illuminator, splashing its luminescence around the walls of the cavern, picking out his path along the floor. There seemed to be no bear, no mutant bear, or any other hostile creature in the cavern. He advanced cautiously, flashing his light ahead of him.

In the distance he thought he spotted a tiny flickering point of light. He doused his pocket illuminator, crouched low, and crept silently toward the point of light.

Slowly the flickering point of light grew, became a flickering campfire. A single figure sat beside the flame, wrapped in a long white robe.

From her own position, farther toward the mouth of the cave, Wilma watched Buck approach the white-robed stranger.

She saw the sitting figure raise its eyes, its meditation interrupted by the arrival of an unexpected visitor. Although Buck was still well out of the range of the campfire's light, the white-robed figure spoke to him: "I sense the presence of a human. Show yourself."

Buck stepped forward, into the glow of the campfire. For a moment Wilma wondered why the cave didn't fill with fumes from the fire, then decided that there must be some second opening through which air flowed. She heard the space-man identify himself, then say, "I am looking for a man named Aris."

"For what purpose do you seek out Aris?" the other asked.

"I need help. I'm looking for my family. Not my personal family—my descendants. It's not an easy thing to explain. But I don't wish you any harm. Honestly."

"Sit," the white-robed figure said. "I am Aris."

Buck lowered himself to a cross-legged position beside Aris' campfire. "I bring you a present from the Inner City," he said, reaching inside his civilian garment and extracting a small parcel. "It's a pair of—in my day, we'd have called them long johns. But supermodern ones. They store solar power. Just put 'em out in the sunlight and they save it up, keep you cozy on a chilly night here in the cave." Buck laughed nervously.

"Are you here to give me underwear, Captain Rogers?" Aris asked.

Buck shook his head. "Er, not really. I just wanted to, ah, make friends. Kind of dumb of me, wasn't it?" He put away the underpants.

"I am 137 years old, Captain Rogers," Aris said. "I don't expect to strike up many more friendships in the time left to me."

"Gotcha!" Buck nodded vigorously. "And how old do you think *I* am, Mr. Aris?"

The old man looked at him. "I'd say, thirty-five or so."

"A little more than that. I'm exactly 537 years old."

The old man looked at Buck silently for a long time. Finally he said, "Pardon my skepticism, but I doubt that that's so."

"Yeah," Buck said. "Well, I haven't exactly *lived* for 537 years. I was *born* 537 years ago. But, ah, I was frozen. You know, those cryogenic things. But by accident. I was sent on a mission in space. Back in 1987. Something went wrong with my ship, I still don't understand exactly what happened. But I was in suspended animation for five hundred years. I was only supposed to be gone five years. But while I was out there"—he gestured— "the world that *I* knew ended. I don't know what really happened. Something about a holocaust. Dictators . . . bombs . . . nuclear pollution. All over, poof! Wham!

"When I got back, got unfrozen, my world was wrecked. There's no connection between *this* world, today, and the world I knew."

"And yet there were survivors," Aris countered. "A new civilization has begun, as you have seen."

"Yes," Buck agreed. "That's the point. Maybe some of those survivors are related to me. Even just one. If I could find anybody that I was connected with, you see, somehow I wouldn't feel quite so . . . alone in this world."

Aris nodded. "And what if there are none?"

"Even so. Even to know for sure that all of them —my family, my friends—were completely wiped out. Even that would be better than not knowing." He paused. "At least, I think it would."

"I know of a man named Rogers," Aris said slowly. "I knew his father, Rogers, and his grandfather, Rogers. But, since I am not nearly as old as you are"—a strange smile flickered across the old man's visage—"I cannot say that *these* Rogers are related to you."

"Of course," Buck conceded. "I guess I've been chasing shadows." He rubbed his face with his hands, gathered his thoughts for a few seconds. "Aris, is this the end, then? There's no one who can help me, is that right? So I click my glass slippers together and find happiness right in my own backyard."

Old Aris looked puzzled. "Are you all right? Your speech seems to be becoming muddled."

"Never mind," Buck said. "I think I'd better just beat it out of here. Sorry I bothered you, Aris. Go back to sniffing your campfire smoke or whatever you do to pass the time around here."

He rose to his feet and started to make his way back to the entrance of the cave.

Wilma Deering, seeing Buck headed for her hiding place, scrambled out of the cave ahead of him. She scurried away from the cave mouth and began to run toward the landcar. Suddenly a group of figures rose, as if from the Earth itself, surrounding Wilma. They were dressed as shepherds, and even had the unmistakable odor of sheep to them, but something looked not quite right about them. Something almost inhuman, alien.

Wilma tried to sprint past them, to the landcar, but two massive figures loomed before her. She tried to dodge around them, felt herself seized, started to scream to Buck—half a cry for aid, half a warning to save himself—but before she had got out a single sound she felt the momentarily stun-

ning paralysis of a laser-pistol set to immobilize
without killing.

She slumped into the arms of the massive shepherd—or pseudo shepherd—nearest her, unconscious and limp.

As Buck headed away from Aris' campfire, the
old man called after him. "There is one other place
you might try, my friend."

"Forget it," Buck gritted bitterly. "Thanks anyhow."

He strode away from the campfire, slowed his
pace, halted, turned back. "Where?" he asked.

"I have heard of a great temple," Aris told him,
"a house of God where they have kept records of
families and of tribes over a span of hundreds of
years. It is located by a great white seabed where
the sand tastes strangely of salt. Some of our people go there to bring away the dried salt. But
rarely, for this place is thousands of miles from
here, in the direction of the sunset."

Buck shook his head, trying to unravel the meaning of the old man's directions. Finally he said,
"Salt Lake City?"

"I know not by what name the place is called,
Buck Rogers."

"But it must be," Buck muttered, half to Aris
and half to himself. "The old Mormon Temple.
They were always doing work on genealogy. They
even had it computerized, way back in the twentieth century. If they're still in business—Aris,
you're a genius!"

He sprinted from the cave and started down
the hill toward his landcar. He approached the
car, halted. Suddenly his burst of euphoria dissi-

pated. Something was wrong. He couldn't tell what it was, but—and then he could. There was evidence of strangers, of shepherds.

There were footprints near his car, and on a grassy patch he could even see their flock grazing. Beyond the meadow he could see the bushes thickening and even a stand of thick-growing trees that stretched into the foothills and low mountains nearby.

But—not a soul was visible!

Buck sprinted to his car. He bent to see if anyone was hiding inside it, waiting to ambush him. Instead they came from the opposite side of the car, diving across its low, curved roof, swinging hamlike fists at Buck from either side. He bounded aside, let the two false shepherds pound their fists onto each other. Before they could recover their equilibrium and return to the attack, Buck was on them, pounding his fists against their jaws, driving one solid punch after another into their torsos. If there was any way that one tough man could take two, Buck would have succeeded. But instead a third figure emerged from hiding and aimed a laser-pistol point-blank at the daring spaceman.

The new arrival squeezed the trigger on his weapon and Buck Rogers dropped to the ground —but not as a result of the bolt of force that the weapon spewed at him. Some subtle warning, some sixth sense that separates the extraordinary man from the ordinary had warned him of peril from a new direction.

The bolt singed the billowing robe of one of the shepherds Buck had been fighting. Rogers hit the ground, spun, and launched himself through the air straight at his newest assailant. Buck's muscular shoulder caught the newcomer squarely in the solar plexus, knocking the wind out of him with a single powerful *whoosh*.

Buck whirled again, saw that the man was doubled over in pain but still clutched his handweapon. Meanwhile the other two would-be assassins had drawn lasers of their own.

Buck set a zigzag course away from the band of assailants, headed for the scrubby bushes nearby, then dodged left and right with the same speedy agility that had made him a football star on the Space Academy's varsity eleven five-hundred-odd years before. Half-expecting to be brought down at any moment by a laser-bolt, he heaved a sigh of relief as he made it into the thick woods at the edge of the meadow.

He plunged into the trees, dodging left and right so that thick trunks stood between himself and the pursuing pseudo shepherds at all times. After a while he leaped for an overhanging limb, swung himself onto it and scooted sideways to the trunk of the tree. He placed one foot in a crotch of the trunk, pulled himself into it, raised his body to a higher limb and stood, crouching against the main trunk of the tree, watching the helpless pursuit that went on below.

Finally he saw the false shepherds headed back in the direction from which they had come.

They disappeared. In a few minutes he heard their voices raised in loud disagreement, then the slamming of doors and the purr of a landcar engine. Buck remained in his tree until he was sure they were gone, then descended to the ground and began to calculate. He had escaped from his assailants and he had a good clue—at least, one that could raise his hopes—to getting some information on his family.

But he had lost his groundcar, and he was stranded here in what had been South Dakota. He had to make his way back to Chicago. Could he survive the journey?

There was only one way to find out!

CHAPTER 7.

The shimmering dome of the Inner City seemed to waver and dance before his eyes, to fade into insubstantiality and then to come back to sharp, glowing existence. The walls that surrounded the city itself, nestled securely beneath the dome, loomed seemingly higher than mountains, insuperable barriers that no expenditure of effort could cross.

The man who stumbled and drove himself mercilessly across the last few hundred yards was ragged, bearded, sun-baked, emaciated. But even his fatigue-bleared eyes remained fixed on his objective. He fell forward, catching himself with sun-browned, sinewy hands on the towering wall, and with his last remaining strength of muscle pounded on the unyielding surface, demanding entry into the city.

At the same time he shouted hoarsely for the city guards to come and admit him into the dome.

A panel opened and a team of Inner City guardsmen strode into the afternoon sunlight, smart and precise in their military-cut regulation garb. They took the ragged figure by its elbows and brought it into the city, as much carrying as guiding it along the way.

Half delirious with fatigue and exposure, Buck Rogers found himself in a light-cell, a futuristic holding location where the guardsmen had placed him. There were no walls as such around him, no bars such as had been used to hold prisoners in the days of his youth. Instead, barriers of pure radiation, coruscating light, and tingling electromagnetic force held him as securely as would have brick walls or iron bars.

He sat morosely contemplating his situation.

After an unmeasured time had elapsed the light-wall drew back to reveal an opening the size and shape of a doorway, save for its shimmering, glittering edges.

In the lucent oval of the opening there stood a diminutive figure, bald-headed, pink-skinned, gimlet-eyed, wearing a white laboratory smock and a pair of glinting, old-fashioned spectacles. Buck knew that Dr. Huer was virtually the only man who still affected glass disks and metal earpieces in this age when permanently implanted minilenses could give any man or woman lifelong perfect vision, provided only that nature had provided them with a functioning retina and optic nerve.

Dr. Huer advanced into the light-cell. The pseudo doorway drew shut behind him.

Diminutive as he was, Huer stood over the form of Buck who slumped despondently on the floor of his cell.

"I have only one thing to ask you, Buck," the old scientist said in mild, low tones. Then, his voice rising surprisingly to a near shout, "What the hell is going on?"

Startled from his somnolence, Buck struggled to answer. "Hey, I didn't mean anything," he said. "I just wanted to find some trace of my family. Sorry I lost a landcar, you can take it out of my salary. Come to think of it, Doc, what does a rock-jock in the Inner City defense squadron get paid any-how? I've been around this place for a while now, and I always seem to have enough petty cash to get by on, but when does the eagle really fly?"

"Eagle fly? What are you talking about?" Huer asked.

"I mean—oh, never mind. I was just asking when payday comes around. I guess I'll really have to pay for that landcar I lost."

"The landcar isn't the only thing you lost," Huer voiced firmly.

"It isn't?" Buck echoed.

"No, it certainly isn't," Dr. Huer supplied.

"Oh, let me think," Buck rubbed his temples. After a few seconds the expression on his haggard face altered. "Oh, yeah—I do remember now."

"I'm glad you do."

"Yeah, Doc. I'm really sorry. Those computer brains must really be expensive. I'm sorry that I traded it away—I guess it'll take me a while to pay that off. But I'll make a start this very first pay-day."

Huer shook his head despairingly. "I'm not talk-ing about any piece of machinery, Captain Rogers. Are you not aware that Colonel Deering has also failed to return?"

"Colonel Deering? You mean Wilma? Wilma's

missing?" Buck pushed himself up on his elbows, struggled to his feet despite the weakness that almost brought him crashing again to the floor. This was the first real animation Buck had shown since Huer's arrival in his cell. "But what does Wilma have to do with it?" Rogers asked.

"I'm afraid she's been captured, Buck. She's very likely in the hands of enemies—if she's still alive at all."

"Doc! This is terrible! We have to do something about this." Buck was weaving back and forth, as he forced his weary body to stay upright. "We have to get her back!

"But—Doc, Wilma Deering wasn't with me. I went out of the city—I know it was against orders. I was trying to find some evidence of my family. But I was all alone."

"Yes, Buck, we know that. But what *you* seem not to know is that Colonel Deering cares about you very deeply. She was very worried over your mysterious conduct, and she followed you to find out where you were going—and why.

"Now, listen to me," Huer's eyes bored into Buck's, even through the old scientist's thick-lensed spectacles. "You've got to help me figure this out, Buck. And we can worry about the other matters later. Buck, based on your own travels, have you any idea where Wilma might have become lost—or injured—or captured?"

Buck took his head in his hands and tugged at his hair as if to pull an answer through his skull. "Yes!" he exclaimed. "I've got it! It must have been those shepherds. Or—phony shepherds."

"What shepherds, Buck? There are no shepherds anywhere near the Inner City."

"I know that, Doc. This was at the old Mount Rushmore Memorial. Way back, even before my day, some sculptor carved the faces of four former presidents of the United States into the side of a mountain out in South Dakota. I found out that there was a man living near there. An old, old man named Aris, who might be able to help me with the information I was after.

"I took a landcar and drove there to find Aris. I did, too—living in a cave right under the memorial. When I got back to my landcar there were some strange-looking shepherds hanging around, and—"

Dr. Huer interrupted his narration. "What do you mean by 'strange-looking,' Buck? They were human, weren't they?"

Buck frowned, recalling the faces he had seen briefly in his battle with the pseudo sheepherders. "They were human," he said, "but they looked somehow—unearthly. I'm pretty sure they must have been—Draconians! I didn't think of it at the moment, everything was happening so fast, Doc— but I'm sure, now, that they were definitely Draconians!"

"And you think they took Wilma?" Huer prodded.

"They must have! They got her, if she was there. And they got my landcar, too! I had to walk all the way back to the Inner City. That's why I was gone so long—and it nearly killed me, into the bargain."

"I see, I see." Now it was Huer's turn to become

agitated. He paced up and down, impatiently turning every time he reached the limit of the cell's light-wall. "All right, Buck," he stopped his pacing. "There's only one course to follow. We've got to organize a rescue expedition and head back to Mount Rushmore."

"That wouldn't do any good," Buck countered. "I'm sure those shepherds wouldn't be there any more. In fact, I heard them leave in my own landcar before I started my walk back here.

"If Wilma overheard my conversation with old Aris—or if the Draconians found Aris and questioned him themselves—then the only place they'd be is—Salt Lake City!"

"What's that? I never heard of such a city."

"It's a place where there was a genealogical-records center. Old Aris knew about it. The shepherds would know that I was headed there. They might have Wilma there, or if they've taken her elsewhere—maybe even somewhere off-planet—I've still got to go to Salt Lake. That's where *they* would be looking for *me*. Now I've got to play into their hands, or seem to, so they can lead me to wherever they've taken Wilma!"

"I don't know, Buck," Huer shook his head doubtfully. "The more complex your scheme grows, the less I find myself liking it."

"Doc, we've got to! It's the only chance!"

"Well—" Huer paused, deep in thought. Finally he yielded. "All right, I'll concede this much. I'll take it up with my personal counselor. I'll consult the greatest computer brain yet constructed. Dr. Theopolis."

"No, Doc," Buck said sadly.

Huer looked up from his mood of concentration. "No, you say?"

"No." Buck shook his head.

"Why not?"

"Because Theopolis isn't here any more. I was just starting to tell you that when you changed the subject. I'm afraid that I traded him to a gypsy named Pandro for the information that Aris was still alive and could help me with my quest."

"Oh, my, oh, my," Huer said over and over. "Then I'm afraid that my only other course will have to be to appeal to the full council. And when I do that, and they hear of your escapades and the way you lost both Wilma and Theopolis, they're going to be very upset with me—and very, very, *very* upset with you, Buck!"

The Inner City Council of Computers met in a secure chamber in the heart of the Palace of Mirrors. There were levels and degrees of security clearance to be passed through before anyone could begin to approach the council chamber, and by the time anyone reached the chamber itself, he had passed the ultimate tests of loyalty and reliability of the Inner City—or had been dragged there unwillingly, a prisoner brought to face the bar of justice.

In today's proceeding, Dr. Huer and Captain Buck Rogers had given their testimony and then been excused while the computer brains went to their private deliberations. Each brain was a device of data circuits and processor arrays, microminiaturized storage units and advanced-logic pathways. All were similar, and all were housed

in like plexiglass cases, but in their innermost circuitry no two were quite identical. It was as if a
council of the wisest of human minds had assembled: all alike in outer form (more or less)
and all alike in inner function (also more or less),
but all unique as well, each the individual product
of a special combination of heredity and environment unlike, in whatever great or small manner,
the others.

Their names hardly mattered.

Their backgrounds, their unique capabilities,
were hidden inside those identical plexiglass cases.

But their deliberations sounded like this:

"The man is a menace. He should be banned
from the city."

"No, that's too good for him. He has lost the
commander of our finest fighter squadron, and the
most complex and advanced computer advisor in
our own ranks—our very good friend and colleague Theopolis."

"We must be rational about this. After all, we
are computers ourselves, not protoplasm beings like
the humans. The question before us is this: shall
we allow Captain Rogers to go to this Salt Lake
City place, and perhaps be taken prisoner by the
Draconians, in the hopes of retrieving Colonel
Deering or Dr. Theopolis?"

"No! We must simplify matters. Deering and
Theopolis are lost! We had best keep Rogers a
prisoner and prevent his doing still more harm!"

"Now, wait, my friends. What will best serve
the Inner City? That must be our prime guiding
principle in all things. This man is from the

twentieth century. His knowledge of the past is a unique resource. Further, he is a born pilot, an expert rocket flyer. He is too valuable to waste, sitting and rotting in a light-cell."

"On the other hand, Colonel Deering and Dr. Theopolis are also valuable members of the city —too valuable to let go of without at least an attempt to regain them. This man is our only link to their disappearance and our hope for getting them back! We have to let him try, for the good of the city."

"That does compute, doesn't it?"

"I'm afraid it does. I dislike doing so, but I fear I have to agree."

"Yes, I agree also."

"Very well, then, we have reached our consensus. The council is agreed that Rogers will be freed—not cleared of the charges against him, but rather offered his freedom as an opportunity to go after the others and try to rescue one or both of them!"

Buck was sitting in Dr. Huer's office when word of the council's decision arrived. He had been cleaned up since his arrival back at the Inner City and his incarceration in the light-cell. His hair was combed now, his face smooth-shaven, his tattered rags replaced by a sleek set of male garb.

His tormented body had been rebuilt by good eating and special nutrient supplements. He was strong and spry, ready to return to whatever action presented itself.

Dr. Huer received the official notification of the

council's command and informed Buck of it. "I'm not thrilled," the aged savant commented. "You're neither convicted nor cleared, Buck. You're to be freed conditionally, in hopes of getting back Wilma and Theopolis."

"Good," Rogers snapped. "I don't care what kind of official stamp those boxes of dry cells put on my papers. The important thing is that they're willing to let me go after Wilma."

Huer stared at Buck.

"And Theopolis," the latter added. "I miss Theo, too, Doc. But after all, he *is* just a machine!"

"I'm not sure that I'd agree with you on that point," Dr. Huer countered, "and I doubt very much that Dr. Theopolis would! But—as soon as Ellis 14 arrives with your special equipment, we can start getting you ready to go."

"Who's Ellis 14?" Buck asked.

"Why, he's here now," Huer replied, as a panel slid open in the wall and a tall figure emerged from it.

Ellis 14 was as tall as Buck Rogers. He had a shimmering metallic skin, a slim but powerful build, and a graceful, confident way of moving himself. He was a sort of male analogue of the female secretarial robot in the outer office, Lisa 5.

"How do you do, Captain Rogers," Ellis 14 said in an electronic voice. "I'm very pleased to make your acquaintance."

"Likewise," Buck mumbled, not certain whether it was etiquette to offer to shake hands with a robot.

"I'm your armorer," Ellis 14 intoned. "I've

brought you some equipment for use on your new mission. Here," he said, extending a laser-gun toward Buck, hilt first, "your personal hand-weapon. Please be careful with it. Please do not point it at any person or object you do not mean to destroy. That includes me. It is capable of cutting through twelve senks of alum."

Buck took the pistol and slipped it into his belt.

Ellis 14 held a small, soft case toward Buck. "This is your survival kit," the robot said. "It contains first-aid devices as well as signaling and survival gear. Notable features are the blood-stop, brace clamp, emergency protein supply, moisture synthesizer, and solar-storage blanket."

"I wish I'd had this on my way back from Rushmore," Buck commented.

"That is regrettable," the robot answered. "The kit is a non-sensitive item and would have been available to you upon request, Captain Rogers. Why did you not draw one before departing Inner City?"

"Never mind," Buck said. "How's about a spare pair of socks?"

"Notice the linear extrusions on the outer surface of the survival kit," Ellis 14 answered. "Emergency clothing supplies contained therein are made to expand upon contact with outer atmosphere and/or vacuum to counteract the special contractile storage conditions of the container."

"I'm sorry I asked," Buck said huskily.

"Also," Ellis 14 said, "here is your line-beam." He handed Buck a tiny package hardly bigger than a .22-caliber cartridge. "Hide this anywhere upon your person, or leave it in a place of your own selection for alternate usage. It is a line-transmitting device which emits a unique pulsating signal which we can detect and locate from selected monitoring stations. Its range is indefinite and its speed of propagation, as yet unmeasured, appears to approach the instantaneous."

"What's he talking about, Doc?" Buck asked Dr. Huer.

"What he's saying, Buck, is that if you keep that line-beam on your person, we can locate you, at any time, any place in the known universe. Or, if you leave it somewhere else, we can locate the line-beam itself."

"Ah-*hah!*" Buck commented. "O-*kay!* You guys have some hotshot equipment section around here. You've come a long way since old oh-oh-whatsizname's day!"

The door from Dr. Huer's reception room opened and the Lisa 5 secretarial robot entered the inner office. She handed a message to Dr. Huer. "I'm sorry to interrupt, Doctor. I think this may be very urgent."

Huer accepted the scrap of message paper from the robot.

Meanwhile Buck was watching a bit of amazing interplay between the Lisa 5 and the Ellis 14 robots. As the secretarial model entered the room the armorer had followed her every move with the electro-optical scanners that he used for eyes.

While Dr. Huer was reading the message form, Lisa 5 looked around the inner office. When her eyes—or electro-optical scanners—met Ellis 14's, an almost visible bolt of energy passed between the two slim figures. In an instant Lisa 5 looked away, for all the world like a shy, yet subtly coquettish woman noticing the frank admiration of an attractive man.

Huer looked up from the message slip. Absent-mindedly he thanked the Lisa 5 robot again for bringing it. Then to Buck he said, "This is a report on the playback scan of the Mount Rushmore area. We had it shot from orbit. I'm sorry, Buck, it doesn't show anything very useful."

Lisa 5 had remained standing near Dr. Huer— and Ellis 14. Now Huer noticed her and said, "Thank you, Lisa. You may go."

She exchanged a parting glance with Ellis 14 that all but singed the air between them to an electric-blue cinder—then moved back to the outer doorway, swaying as she went.

"I wonder if that was passion or just a short circuit," Buck laughed.

Huer, abstractedly again, simply hummed.

"How do these robots reproduce?" Buck asked softly.

"We build them in a factory. How did you think?" Huer responded.

"Maybe you don't have to."

Ellis 14 said, "Captain Rogers, you should have a soma drone to replace your broken Twiki, and a new compuvisor to replace Dr. Theopolis."

"Don't worry about it," Buck told the armorer. "I want to travel light on this little outing. I'll go alone. And I intend to get Theo back. He thinks I sold him out—and I suppose I did, in a way. But

if I'm responsible for his loss, then I'll be the one
to rescue him, too!"

"I hope you're right, Buck," Dr. Huer remarked.
His voice, and his face, were those of a very worried man.

CHAPTER 8.

Fully outfitted in a military g-suit—or the twenty-fifth-century equivalent of that marvelous invention of Buck Rogers' own era—and with all the special gear that Ellis 14 had provided him, Buck sat aboard a flashing monorail car, headed from his quarters in a smart residential sector of the Inner City, to the defense squadron ready-area of the domed metropolis' spaceport.

His head was filled with his worries and his plans. The loss of Wilma Deering—and her presumed capture by the Draconians—had brought home to Buck the true strength of his feelings for her. These weren't just the loyalty of a rocket jockey for his commanding officer, although that was part of Buck's feeling; nor merely a sense of the obligations of friend-and-colleague for a fellow member of the spacefaring fraternity, although that was part of Buck's feeling, too.

There was a stronger sensation than either of those familiar emotions. It was something that made his belly feel warm, his chest tight, and his head light whenever he thought of Wilma. It was something that Buck had heard about, read about, seen movies about, sung songs about—yet never quite believed in until now.

"Yep," he thought to himself, "in the words of the immortal Duke Ellington tune, I got it bad and that ain't good!"

He leaped to his feet as the monorail slid to a silent halt at the Inner City spacefield. He climbed down from the train and platform, passed through the ready-room, and crossed the tarmac, stepping between the waiting, ever-ready fighter rockets that stood prepared to blast off in defense of the Inner City and all of Earth at a moment's notice.

He dismissed the ground crewmen who worked efficiently around the starfighters, climbed into the cockpit of his own craft, and dogged down the pilot hatch.

He started through the checklist that every pilot had to follow before any takeoff. As Buck neared the end of the list there was a bleep from his cockpit telescreen. He finished the checklist and flipped the toggle to activate the telescreen.

The screen flickered to life. A face filled its dimensions—a rounded, hairless dome, a face with small, refined, even wizened features and bright, piercing eyes that bored into Buck's from behind a pair of old-fashioned, lens-and-earpiece spectacles.

"Huer here," the cockpit speaker announced unnecessarily.

"Yes, Doc," Buck answered.

"I just 'vised you to wish you—what did you people used to say? *Bon ami!*"

"Thanks, Doc," Buck laughed. "That's French for *good friend*. I think you meant *bon voyage*.

That means *good trip*. But I appreciate the thought, I really do."

"All right, Buck. Try to stay in contact. Use your line-beam any time. And try to bring Wilma back for us, will you?"

"You bet, Doc. And thanks for the call. I don't know why I didn't think of using a starfighter before, for traveling around this continent. With the roads mostly shot and the trains not running any more, it sure beats the tar out of walking a couple of thousand miles."

He flicked off the televisor link with Dr. Huer and switched it for a video scan of the Earth from his starfighter. Then he punched the firing stud for his main power-packs and the ever-present hand of the space god slammed him back against his padded pilot's seat.

The starfighter blasted away from the tarmac, away from the spaceport, away from the Inner City, away from the banks of what had once been Lake Michigan.

Only this time it did not continue into the void of outer space, either to orbit the Earth or to head for some more distant celestial point. It arced, instead, across the heavens over North America, headed in a sub-orbital path from northeast to southwest, to the basin of what had once been the Great Salt Lake and was now a huge, glistening white salt flat in the middle of the great southwestern desert.

In a mere matter of minutes the starfighter completed a journey even longer than the one that had taken Buck so long, when he returned on foot from Mount Rushmore to the Inner City. As the one-man rocket arced in for its landing, Buck hit the manual override switch and took control back from the ship's computer guidance system. He guided the starfighter in for a landing, like a one-time fighter jockey making for the deck of an oceangoing aircraft carrier.

The starfighter skidded to a halt on glistening salt flats and Buck Rogers undogged the pilot hatch, climbed from the cockpit, and hit the hard, dry surface of the old lakebed.

Before him stretched an incredible sight. It was as if he had mistakenly set a course for one of the planet's polar ice caps instead of the heart of old Utah. A sea—or rather, an "ice floe"—of dazzling, pure white stretched as far as the eye could see. Buck started forward and the "ice" crystals crunched drily beneath his flight-booted feet.

And at the far edge of the plain of whiteness there rose what might have been some relic-city left at the South Pole by a prehistoric race of non-human, perhaps even extraterrestrial, intelligence. Its spires rose into the air, some of them sheared off as if by a gigantic scythe, others complete to their tips where statues of golden angels sounded silent trumpets to summon long-dead multitudes to worship.

This strange vision was in the middle of the Utah desert, and the ice floe was really a salt flat, the dried residue of the onetime Great Salt Lake. And the temperature was well over a hundred degrees by the long-abandoned Fahrenheit scale of Captain Buck Rogers' youth.

Buck sealed his starfighter securely and set out across the salt flats. By the time he reached the ancient temple at their far edge he was drenched in perspiration and his heat-sapped muscles were crying out for relief. But he grinned, and he pounded on the towering ornate doors of the temple. There was no response save the echo of Buck's own blows.

"Sure," he muttered to himself. "All dead." But if the files survived . . .

He scanned the ground for a few yards around, found a half-rusted metal bar, and jammed its thin end between the edges of the two great doors. A few heaves of his muscular shoulders, applied to the makeshift pry-bar, and the doors creaked open.

Buck stepped inside.

The inside of the old temple still had an air of splendor for all that its roof and walls were falling in and its once-polished floor was thickly littered with debris and covered with thick dust and wind-blown sand and salt-crystals. Buck wandered through the building until he found a directory hanging crookedly from a single wall-bracket.

He rubbed away the accumulated grime from the covering of the directory and found the words, *Genealogy Section in Basement.* He picked his way through fallen fixtures and rotting rubble until he found a stairway. No point in looking for an elevator—if there was one it would surely be inoperable.

In the basement he found the genealogy section, threw open its doors and stepped into—a completely empty room!

What had happened? No files, no shelves or cabinets or stacks of crumbling papers. No trays of microfiches or racks of computer tapes.

Nothing!

Buck stood, stunned, gazing at the cavernous, vacant vault. Suddenly he was buried under half a dozen muscular bodies. Buck flailed out with arms and legs, struggling to free himself of the grip of his unanticipated assailants. He landed a solid right to the jaw of one attacker, felt a satisfying impact as he planted one foot in the belly of another.

He freed an elbow long enough to land it in the Adam's apple of a third, and over the turmoil and confusion of the free-for-all, heard the man gasping and retching desperately.

An arm clamped around Buck's face, the beefy muscle closing off his nose and mouth in an effort to smother him into submission. He managed to get his teeth open, then clamped them ferociously into the arm. With a howl of outrage his attacker released his grip, yanked the arm away with a sound of tearing cloth—or flesh!

The force of the man's reaction spun Buck out of the grip of his remaining assailants and he sprawled a few yards across the untenanted floor of the room, leaped to his feet and drew his laser-pistol. Before he could get off a single bolt he was dealt a vicious, treacherous rabbit punch from behind. He was stunned, his knees buckling beneath him.

Through dimming eyes he saw a huge Draconian lunging toward him. He managed to squeeze off a bolt at the attacker but the Draconian's momentum carried him forward and he collided with Buck, the two of them collapsing to the floor. A hand reached into the tangle of flaccid limbs and seized Buck's laser-gun. Thick fingers adjusted the setting and another bolt was fired—this time at Captain Buck Rogers!

The gloom and partial unconsciousness that he had been fighting increased, then disappeared into total nothingness.

The giant Draconian starship received the little shuttlecraft into its hangar bay, the movable plates of the bay's outer shell rotating on their gimbal joints as servomotors whined. The hatches of the shuttlecraft swung open as soon as air-pressure indicators showed a safe level of atmosphere inside the bay.

Draconian-uniformed crewmen swarmed around the shuttlecraft as it unloaded. Two of the six Draconians aboard the shuttle were carried out on stretchers, two went toward a debriefing room, and two headed for the first-aid station. The prize prisoner, Buck Rogers, was brought out on a stretcher. He was transferred from stretcher to rolling cart and checked over at once by a Draconian medic, who looked up from his medic-probe readouts and nodded his satisfaction.

On the control bridge of the starship, meanwhile, commands were issued to put the engines of the behemoth into star-warp mode. With an acceleration almost imperceptible to the occupants of the mighty hulk, the ship accelerated past conventional speeds, through the perilous light-speed zone and into warp-space where all of the normal laws of time and dimension are called into question.

As those crewmen brave enough to watch the

normal universe turned inside out gazed in awe
through the viewing ports of the ship's bridge,
Buck Rogers opened his own eyes. They were still
somewhat bleary, his ears still rang and his body
ached and tingled as if it had been struck by a
bolt of lightning—which, in a sense, it had.

The room in which Buck found himself was a
sumptuous stateroom aboard the Draconian ship.
The furnishings were soft, rich, clearly designed
for the pleasure of one whose sensuous impulses
were routinely indulged to the ultimate degree.

And, looming above Buck, the carefully calculated casualness of her posture designed to show
off the luxuriant, tempting curves of a generously
proportioned torso, was the Princess Ardala. Last
unmarried daughter of the Emperor Draco, Ardala was heiress-apparent to the throne of the
greatest interstellar empire in the known history of
the universe.

The Draconian Empire stretched from Canopus
to Tau Ceti, from Ophiuchi to Wolf-35. It took in
stars, planets, and nebulae, worlds of incredible
mineral riches, magnificent wildlife, and intelligences and civilizations so perfectly humanoid that
no earth-born visitor could detect a difference—
as well as some so totally alien that no ordinary
man could look upon them and still retain his
sanity!

The Emperor Draco had fathered thirty children in his lifetime—or, thirty that he was willing
to acknowledge as royal offspring. By an incredible medical anomaly—or perhaps, simply, by a
wildly astonishing run of chromosomes on the

cosmic wheel of fortune—all thirty of the royal offspring were daughters.

Of these, twenty-nine had married. And Draco had found each and every one of his twenty-nine sons-in-law unsatisfactory stock for the breeding of an interstellar imperial dynasty. All had been gently but firmly buried in the administrative bureaucracy of the Draconian Empire, sent to obscure military outposts in positions of grand pomp and no authority, appointed to positions academic or administrative where they and their wives, the imperial princesses, could live out their lives in comfort and honor—but would pose no threat to the throne of the empire.

Draco's last hope was Ardala. She *must* find a mate suitable to father the future emperors of the Draconian realm! *She must!*

Kane, the oily and treacherous satrap of a series of imperial enclaves, had attached himself repeatedly to Ardala's entourage, hoping to ingratiate himself with the princess and establish himself as prince-consort to the heiress-apparent of the empire. Ardala had played with Kane, now leading him on, now rebuffing his overeager advances.

It was only when she first saw Buck Rogers that she understood why she had refused to give her hand to Kane. Here, in this earthman from the past, was the proper consort for Her Highness! As Kane had pursued Ardala, so Ardala now was prepared to all but fling herself at Buck Rogers.

There had been one problem to overcome— reading between the lines of the reports from her spies, Ardala had seen that Rogers had apparently chosen the simpering, scrawny Wilma Deering of Earth.

But the lusty, voluptuous Ardala was by no means giving up on her choice of a consort. Certainly not with Wilma Deering safely out of the way—at least for a time!—and Buck Rogers lying helpless on his back beneath the hot eyes and hotter hands of Princess Ardala!

Rogers managed to focus his eyes, peering helplessly up into the dark, fiery orbs of the princess. As he did so the princess whispered, "Welcome, Buck Rogers. You are in *my* domain now, and I offer you warmest welcome."

Buck blinked. "Princess Ardala," he said at last. "So it *is* you. I thought I was having a dream."

"How nice of you to say so," the princess cooed. She leaned closer to Buck so he could feel her breath on his cheek, her soft, eager torso pressing against his chest.

"It was like—" Buck paused.

"Yes," Ardala prompted, "what was it like, your dream of me?"

"Like—some kind of weird nightmare," Buck said.

The exertion of even the brief dialogue was too much for a man who had survived the strains that Buck Rogers had endured. Once more consciousness slipped from him.

Ardala pulled away from the unconscious man, fury written boldly across her barbarously beautiful features. "A nightmare," she echoed furiously. "A nightmare! You swine! You insolent, worthless dog, Rogers! You shall pay for that insult! You and your pale nothing, your excuse-for-a-sweetheart Deering!

"You shall pay for that, both of you!"

CHAPTER 9.

The Intelligence and Scanning Center of Inner City command headquarters was the second most important and second most secret location in the planetary capital's military establishment. It was second only to the War Room itself. And there were those who maintained, not without good cause, that even this was a reversal of the true situation—that the Intelligence and Scanning Center was actually *more* important than the War Room itself.

Radar screens glowed eerily in the gloomy, cavernous room. Computer terminals clicked and chattered as they printed out status and condition reports on the Earth's military preparedness, on the location and course of every known space-craft within striking range of Earth, of every interceptor ship and weapon in the planet's defensive arsenal.

Things had not always been so on Earth. At one time the planet's military preparedness was divided and directed at other targets on the surface of the planet itself. Nation had stood poised, ready to spring at the throat of nation. Real or imagined enemies glared angrily across polar azimuths, each tensely awaiting a sign that the other was preparing to attack, each ready with a preemptive strike force of its own.

Then had come the holocaust.

And after the holocaust, just as Earth was beginning to recover its strength for a new assault on the heights of civilization, the planet had learned that it needed all its preparedness and all its fighting strength to defend itself against a new menace —the Empire of Draco!

The result had been the construction of Inner City's defense squadron, the War Room, the planetary defense shield, and the Intelligence and Scanning Center.

Now, as teams of male and female technicians clad in form-fitting, trim unisex uniforms crouched over glowing readout screens and diode-generated messages flashed on overhead projector screens, the most highly respected scientific mind and political leader of the Inner City and the entire planet entered the room.

He was a small, unobtrusive man garbed in prosaic white laboratory clothes. His head was as bald and pink as a baby's, but behind his old-fashioned lens-and-earpiece spectacles, the only personal idiosyncrasy he permitted himself, there gleamed bright and gimlet-sharp eyes.

Dr. Huer approached the chief supervisor of the Intelligence and Scanning Center. The supervisor looked up and greeted the familiar form of the scientist, as did a few technicians not too absorbed in their duties to notice. There were faces of every race and age known on the surface of Earth. Most of them were human, a few of them slightly mutated. One non-human face was that of a Tigerman, and another was the sterile, intelligent visage of the armorer robot, Ellis 14.

"Dr. Huer," the supervisor greeted, "come in."

"Thank you, Latner, I'm already in," the scientist responded sharply. "I want to know the status."

Latner turned to a senior technician. "Put the path readout up on the main screen," he commanded.

The technician obeyed. The main projection screen of the Intelligence and Scanning Center flashed into life. Its surface represented a three-dimensional image of deep space. Glowing points of variously colored light appeared and moved slowly across its surface, representing spaceships being tracked by the monitors.

"We traced Captain Rogers' line-beam to the area on Earth that used to be called the Great Salt Lake," Latner explained to Huer. "The lake is long gone but there are still salt flats there.

"At or near the site of the lakebed, Rogers entered a ruined building. Shortly thereafter he left —or was taken from—the building. We suspect that he was taken, unless he's playing a complex game with us, and had prearranged the whole expedition. Because the ship in which he left was very large. At least a C-III, possibly even a D-III class deepspace cruiser.

"Captain Rogers left his own starfighter behind on the salt flat. It has been retrieved. Totally undamaged and ready to fly."

Latner pointed to the screen again. "The cruiser followed the trajectory indicated on the scanning screen, Doctor. If Captain Rogers meant to escape

from Earth, I should think he'd have abandoned
or disabled his line-beam. On the other hand, he
may be leading us on some sort of subtle chase."
He spread his hands helplessly.

Dr. Huer paced back and forth, his hands
clasped in the small of his back. "The size of the
ship suggests Draconians."

"Yes," Latner agreed, "as far as we know only
their ships have D-III capabilities, and hardly anyone else has even C-III."

"Well, then." Huer's eyes snapped a jolt of in-
terrogation at Latner. "What was the final destination of the cruiser?"

Latner made a series of embarrassed, throat-
clearing sounds. "Ah, we don't exactly know that,
Dr. Huer. We lost the line-beam when the ship
was somewhere in the Tri-org galaxy."

"They went extra-galactic?" Huer demanded.

"Yes. And at some point the cruiser's course took
it to a position where a black sun intervened between the line-beam and our scanners. We lost
them, Doctor. We're continuing the scan. Maybe
we'll pick up the beam again, sir."

Huer sighed dishearteningly. "I thought you
people claimed you'd developed a foolproof scanning technique with the line-beam and scanner
setup. What's the matter with you people?"

"Sir, *I* didn't say the line-beam was foolproof.
None of our *people* did. It was the robot that
developed the line-beam, he's the one who claimed
it was foolproof." Latner jerked a thumb angrily
toward Ellis 14.

The robot shrugged his shoulders sheepishly.

The family of planets circling a distant star whose very light, by the time it reaches Earth, is merely part of a galactic shimmer, bears only a slight resemblance to the family of planets circling Earth's own sun. There is no analogue for tiny, sun-baked Mercury. None for giant, gaseous Jupiter. None for beautiful, ringed Saturn. And surely none for warm, life-spawning Earth.

But there is one point of similarity: there is, in each of the two solar systems we are considering, a belt of "asteroids." More properly (the original name was applied through an ancient astronomical misunderstanding) they should be called "planetoids." That is, a hoop-shaped belt of small, planetlike bodies that revolve around their sun in a common orbit, well out between two of the larger planets' orbits.

On one of these miniature worlds circling that alien sun, there stands an astonishing city. The planetoid is too small to retain any natural atmosphere, but thanks to the well-developed technology of races who dwell within the Draconian Empire—whose science had been looted without payment by their conquering masters—this city boasted a comfortable outdoors atmosphere, complete with parks, roadways, and plazas.

In one of the buildings of the city an earthman lay recovering from exposure, assault, and laser-stun. He was Buck Rogers, having been transferred here at the personal command and under the personal supervision of the Princess Ardala, following their brief, unpleasant exchange aboard the Draconian D-III deepspace cruiser.

Emerging from the deep sleep of exhaustion, Buck looked up to see the sensuous form of the Princess Ardala bending over him, gazing solicitously into his eyes.

"Princess Ardala," Buck said. "I had the strangest dream. I said some things in it. . ."

The princess smiled oddly into Buck's face and took a step away from the place where he lay.

"Don't go," Buck asked.

The princess didn't reply.

Buck reached for her, tried to grasp her with one hand. He *thought* he had put his hand on her arm, but he must have misjudged, for his hand passed through the air.

He sat up, reached with both arms, tried to embrace the voluptuous curves of the princess. His arms passed right through her as if she wasn't there.

"Now *this* must be the dream," Buck gasped. "Maybe that was real before and I'm sleeping now. Maybe I'm not even here, is that it?"

"Oh, you're here all right," the princess said. "*I'm* not."

As Buck watched, open-mouthed, the Princess Ardala slowly, slowly faded from view. Just before she disappeared completely Buck made a lunge, a final attempt to embrace her, but his arms passed completely through the space where she had stood.

"I bet you're not much fun on a date," Buck wisecracked.

The almost-invisible Ardala said, "Oh, I'm real enough, Buck. But my body isn't there with you. I'm speaking via a PersonImage, a holographic

projection. You might say that that's what I am—
a hologram."

"Swell," Buck snapped. "And I'm a Methodist.
But I ain't never seen nothin' like that."

"Oh, I'll come by later, Buck. The next time you
see me I'll be there . . . in the flesh." The emphasis
she placed on the final words sent a ripple of
goosebumps running over Buck's body.

Before he could say anything further, the PersonImage had faded into complete invisibility.

"Out-a-sight," Buck exclaimed. Then he caught
onto his own double entendre, laughed and repeated it. "Out-a-sight!"

There was a knock on Buck's door, and the
panel slid aside, admitting a distinguished-looking
elderly man before Buck had time even to call a
summons to him to enter. The man bowed slightly,
stepped into the room, and said, "Good day, Captain Rogers. I hope you do not mind receiving
visitors."

"Why should I talk to you?" Buck snapped back.
"You're not really here. I've been through all of
that with Ardala. I mean, with Ardala's Person-
Image."

"Oh, I see. Well, I assure you, Captain, that I
am *really* here." The newcomer walked to Buck's
side and said, "Here, try me and see." He held out
his arm in front of Buck.

The earthman tested the other's arm and chest
with both hands, making good and certain that
he was really present and not merely a holographic
projection before he would accept that reality.

"Okay," Buck finally admitted. "So you're really here and she really isn't. I have all the luck."

"Welcome to Villus Beta," the older man smiled.

"Is that on Draconia?" For the first time, Buck's interest was piqued, not merely in terms of his personal being but in terms of his surroundings.

The older man shook his head. "No, this is hardly Draconia. Although of course we are part of the Draconian Empire here. This is an asteroid, dubbed simply Beta, in the Villus solar system. I believe you are a native of the planet Earth. From your home world, you could locate Villus by sighting along the maximum axis of your own Milky Way galaxy. Villus is—oh, I see that you're not yet familiar with extragalactic astrogation. Well, never mind, that will all come to you later. If you want it to.

"For the moment," he strode a few paces away from Buck, turned and stood facing the earthman seriously, "a little information at a time should suffice.

"I am Professor Von Norbert. This"—he made a sweeping gesture with his hands, that might indicate anything from the room where he stood to the entire planetoid—"is where I conduct my experiments. Come along with me, Captain Rogers, and I shall give you a little tour of the facilities."

Why not, Buck thought. He might learn something useful, pick up some clue to the whereabouts of Wilma Deering or Dr. Theopolis. At worst, it would kill a little time. He had nothing better to do around here, so he might as well spend his time learning whatever he could learn.

The entire city of Villus Beta—its name was an

amalgam of the names of the star that gave it light and the planetoid it stood on—was constructed in the form of a gigantic inverted wedge. It stood with its narrow edge pointed skyward, its broad base resting on the surface of the planetoid to provide a stable grounding for its massive weight.

One wall of the city stood against an even more massive natural formation, a cliff of the native rock of the planetoid Beta.

Emerging from the side and base of the inverted wedge closest to the wall of rock were great tunnels. A second bank of these crossed the city at a level halfway from its base to its apex; a thick, level surface had been laid lengthwise along the tops of the later cross-members. The ends of the wedge were open, so that a person standing on the surface of the planetoid Beta would be confronted with a titanic, overwhelming capital letter A.

And the crossbar of the letter A—the level surface that traversed the city from one end to the other—was a single, gigantic spaceport!

Buck stood in awe as Professor Von Norbert showed him the layout of the city.

After they had inspected the general geography of Villus Beta, Buck was permitted to inspect the series of cross-members connecting the base of the city with the wall of rock beside which it was constructed. Here he stood again in awestruck silence.

Here was the greatest accumulation of genetic data and genealogical records in the Draconian Empire—in the known universe! Professor Norbert showed Buck towering banks of computer modules and molecular storage banks where files and indexes of records were stored, where a single inquiry entered through a computer's typewriter-like keyboard or even spoken into a specially activated microphone would send a series of electronic impulses cascading through bank after bank of storage units, file after file of historical records, until a complete history of whatever particular individual, family, or genetic grouping was desired, had been compiled.

At the delivery of another keyed instruction this history could be sorted, edited, sequenced, arranged in any manner desired, then printed out or spoken in an electronically synthesized voice.

In one section of the great computer installation, workers were putting the finishing touches on a new segment of files and processing equipment that had recently been delivered to Beta from Earth. Buck gasped when he saw the markings and insignia on the computers and the filing equipment.

"That's the Mormon Temple records establishment!" he exclaimed.

"Correct," Von Norbert agreed.

"How did it get here?"

"We Draconians are already the greatest genetic researchers in the galaxy. We're just adding one more capability to our already established position of leadership," Norbert explained happily.

"But"—Buck's face darkened with outrage—"what right had you—who gave you permission to land on Earth and haul away property that doesn't even belong to you?"

Von Norbert laughed. "Captain Rogers, I had thought better of you. You are concerned with such petty considerations as trivial legalisms. We are acting in the interests of science, Captain. Ours is a long and noble tradition, stretching back even to your own century, to the genetic experiments carried out in some of the central European locales in the 1940s."

"But—Earth's defense shield!"

Von Norbert shrugged.

Buck—a twentieth-century man—knew, more vividly than any of these twenty-fifth century persons, what those experiments had been in the 1940s. Buck struggled to regain his composure, to keep himself from lashing out with balled fists at this man whose very attitude was an affront to dignity and independence, whose activities in the name of science were an insult to every decent and ethical man and woman of science who had worked to add to the sum of human knowledge over the millennia of civilization's painful rise.

When he felt he could speak calmly and contain his sense of outrage, Buck said, "What kind of experiments do you carry out here on Villus Beta, Doctor?"

They were sitting now in what amounted to a sidewalk cafe. Graceful shafts and curves of colored plexiglass filled with lighted gases provided a strange, almost surrealistic illumination.

"We are striving to combine our modern knowledge of genetics with our researches into genealogy, Captain Rogers. You can see how this will work to the benefit of humanity. We are searching the files of all conquered planets and peoples for those individuals, those families, whose genetic characteristics are most desirable in the race of mankind.

"We do not discriminate by planet of origin. Draconian or earthling, it matters not to us. By combining those positive characteristics, I will create a race of super-positively endowed individuals. This is a dream that mankind has had for thousands of years: the creation of super-man!"

"Sounds more like some stockman trying to breed a stronger strain of horses to me," Buck commented.

"Ah, Captain Rogers, Captain Rogers, do not be so narrow-minded. I realize that your background is unique among all persons living today. You were raised in an age almost barbaric compared to our own. You must learn to adapt yourself to modern ideas."

"Well, what are you shooting for?" Buck demanded.

"We are striving for nothing less than the perfect race. Think of it!" Von Norbert's eyes glowed as he spoke. "To eliminate all genetically-transmitted diseases! To dispose of all who manifest intellectual inferiority! To build a race of the highest stamina, resistance to infection, muscular strength, intellectual acumen, artistic sensitivity, creativity. . ."

As Von Norbert's voice trailed off into his little dream world, three absolutely breathtaking young women strolled past his and Buck's table in the cafe. All of them, clearly, were familiar with Professor Von Norbert, and paused briefly to exchange hellos with him.

The professor was called back from his dream

world by the presence of the young women, whose obviously ripe charms were more than revealed by the skimpy, diaphanous costumes that they affected in the Draconian fashion.

"Hildy," Von Norbert identified the last of the three as the young women strolled on their way. "Well, Buck, what do you think of these results of my experimentation? Is my genetic engineering and selective breeding program such a terrible thing? Are those not specimens of beauty to delight the connoisseur?"

Buck managed to tear his eyes away from the three retreating beauties. "You're out to create a master race, Professor Von Norbert."

"Hmph. Not quite my choice of words, Captain. I am not a serious student of history. My time has been too filled with the study of science. But I believe that the term *master race*, in itself innocuous, carried certain negative political implications in your day."

"It did, Professor," Buck agreed ironically, "it certainly did."

"But leaving aside the political aspect," Von Norbert continued, "a master race is exactly what I *am* creating. Yes, you are entirely correct on that point."

He rose from his seat at the cafe table and took Buck by the elbow, resuming his guided tour of the city.

Buck said, "A little more study of history might be useful for you, Prof. Yes, some people in my century did try something like that. It was a trifle before my personal time, but it was the twentieth century all right.

"Some of the stuff they said sounded okay. In fact, it could have been the same line you were putting out a few minutes ago. That stuff about eliminating physical inferiority and intellectual deficiencies and building a new race of people. It sounded okay, yeah.

"But what it led to was mass murder. Complete disregard for the rights of others. The worst examples of brutality and savagery known in the annals of a world where murder, brutality, and savagery were all too common. Torture, extermination camps, inhumanity on a scale you can hardly imagine.

"Or maybe you can." He glared into the eyes of the other. "And maybe it just doesn't bother you a bit."

Von Norbert laughed aloud. "You're a born reactionary, my boy. Of course I should expect that kind of response from you, your thought processes were formed five hundred years ago."

"Yeah, I guess my thought processes *were* formed five hundred years ago. But then, so was the rest of me. For better or for worse, Professor, that's the way I am—as we used to say way back in the 1980s, that's where I'm coming from!"

"You find creating repugnant, Rogers," the professor charged. "How can you do so, compared to the blowing up and the poisoning of Earth that were committed by your people—by your century? Now *that* is the kind of activity that I find repugnant, not an attempt to free mankind from the dead hand of inherited deficiencies."

"God, we screwed things up in my day, I can't deny that, Prof! I certainly can't defend the wars and the poisoning of the world that we did. But at least we didn't do it as a matter of policy. It was our weaknesses, our failings, our mistakes—not our goals! I wasn't for war, believe me." Buck lapsed into a half-audible tone, speaking more to himself than to Von Norbert. "I wasn't even for Nixon. But then I never could find anybody who admitted that he was!"

"What are you talking about?" Von Norbert asked. He halted and faced Buck.

"I'm sorry," Buck said. "Sort of daydreaming. Must not be as fully recovered from everything that's happened to me as I thought I was. Maybe I'm suffering from something like jet lag, too."

"Well, would you rather rest than continue?" Von Norbert asked.

Buck thought for a moment. If he had roused the professor's sympathy he might be able to gain an advantage, a break that wouldn't be available to him later on. "Back there at the research center," Buck said.

"Yes?"

"I saw the Mormon records."

"Yes, we discussed those, did we not?"

"We discussed your right to take them from Earth, not what use is going to be made of them. Are you just piling up all the data you can find—or do you have some particular use for them?"

"Oh," Von Norbert said, "they are very valuable genealogical records. They are already being put to use, helping us to choose the specimens for our experiments."

Buck was thunderstruck. "And Wilma's a specimen?" he demanded.

"Wilma?" Von Norbert repeated. "You mean Colonel Deering? But no, Captain Rogers, not at all. Colonel Deering seems to be a well-developed young woman, but it is *you* who fascinate me as an experimental subject, my boy. You!"

Suddenly the whole bizarre sequence of events that had led Buck from the Inner City to Anarchia, to the gypsy camp, the dry flats of the Great Salt Lake, and then through space to Villus Beta, fell into place. Now it began to make sense at last!

"You are a most intriguing specimen," Von Norbert confirmed. "That's why we went to considerable inconvenience just to get you here to our facility."

"Damn it!" Buck exploded. "The whole thing was set up. Pandro the gypsy. Aris the old hermit. How in hell did you get people like that onto your payroll? How did you buy them out?"

"We didn't have to," Von Norbert sneered. "They were on our side to start with. They are both actors whom we planted. Even the children in the old Hall of Records—"

"No!"

"But, yes!"

"How could you—?"

"The how of it is not my concern," Von Norbert said. "My work is right here on Villus Beta, and is of a purely scientific nature. Outside operations, including the procurement of experimental specimens"—he reached and prodded Buck's muscular torso with one appraising finger—"are left in the capable hands of persons better qualified to carry them out.

"I have the impression that this particular operation was planned and executed by Kane himself. Under the watchful guidance of the Princess Ardala, of course."

He chuckled enigmatically.

CHAPTER 10.

They had continued to stroll, sporadically, throughout their entire long conversation. Now they arrived at a grand building fitted with ornate architectural furbelows strangely out of keeping with the functional plasticity of the rest of Villus Beta.

Von Norbert threw open a great filigreed door and ushered Buck into a monstrous hall dominated by a single piece of furniture, a huge carved throne whose style managed to combine in one a sense of the twenty-fifth century and of the tenth —a combination of the contemporary and of the archaic. It would have half-fit into any setting in the civilized universe—and half-fit any place in the *un*civilized universe!

Lolling upon it, swathed in a fur-and-satin outfit that looked almost effeminate in its sensuous self-indulgence, was the oily-featured, smug, would-be consort of the crown princess of Draconia: Kane.

As Buck and Professor Von Norbert entered the hall, Kane's eyes lit up with anticipation and pleasure. "Why, hello, Buck Rogers," Kane roared. "If it isn't my good old friend from Earth. And I do mean old—ah, ha-ha-ha-ha-ha-ha!!!" Kane roared with laughter, almost falling from his throne onto the polished plastic-marble floor of the hall.

"Kane!" Buck spat the word. "I should have known. Are you trying to even an old score with all of this?"

"Not at all," Kane cooed preciously. "I *like* you, Rogers."

"Then why did you go to such elaborate means to get me here? Why that band of phony gypsies with their weird old-fashioned CB radio jargon? And why that phony old guru in the cave under Mount Rushmore?"

"Why, Rogers, what do you mean, phony this and phony that?"

"Von Norbert here tells me those were all a bunch of actors."

"Oh, no," Kane disagreed. "The professor doesn't understand anything but science. We wouldn't use phonies, Cap. Pandro is a free agent. He'll work for the highest bidder, any time. But Draconia is usually the high bidder, that's all.

"As for Aris," Kane waved his hand like a holy man gesturing airily, "he's strictly straight-arrow, Rogers. We just figured out what he was likely to tell you, once Pandro sent you to see him. We guessed where he'd send you, and we made it our job to get there first and set up a little welcoming party for you, that's all.

"As for picking you out as an experimental subject, Cap, neither I nor the prof here did that. The computer did. Ain't that the truth, Professor?"

Von Norbert agreed. "Absolutely, Kane. Rogers,

lights and bells went off when we ran your tissue samples through the analyzer. If we'd rejected you, why, I think our computer would have blown a fuse in frustration." He grinned—it was the scientist's idea of a hilarious joke.

"We were after you for a long time, Buck-o," Kane resumed. "You remember your visit to the *Draconia*—when we fished you out of that interplanetary deep-freeze of yours? That was when we took our tissue samples. After that things started popping like all hell broke loose, so we didn't get around to analyzing the samples till later on. By the time you recovered from your big snooze, the little scraped place where we took the specimens must have healed all up. I won't even tell you where it was."

Kane chuckled sinisterly.

"Think of it, Buck-o," the oily courtier went on, "after that big blow-up, when the *Draconia* got wiped—a pity, that. Good ship. I've many a fond memory of disciplining crew members and interrogating prisoners aboard her. But when Ardala and I made good our escape in the mini-pod, just about the only freight we had the time and space to haul away with us was that precious little chunk of your hide. Ah, ha-ha-ha-ha-ha!!!"

Professor Von Norbert resumed his part of the conversation. "When the samples were analyzed and run through the computer, the machine absolutely danced a jig! As far as our preliminary tests can tell, at least, you possess an antibody in your system that has been missing from the human body for hundreds of years. It seems to have occurred only in Earth humans to start with—and to have died out even among them in the period between your first lifetime and your revival.

"You are a unique resource of the state, and as such will be cared for and kept in comfort—but you must also give your unquestioning loyalty to the state that cares for you."

Buck glared at Von Norbert, then at Kane. "Sez you two, maybe. But nobody invited me here—I was dragged in by the heels. I don't think I owe your people anything. And besides, what's so hot about some antibody in my blood? You mean, if I don't share, everybody around here is gonna come down with Virus X next sniffles season?"

"It's no joking matter," Kane roared. "The Draconian race has given too much to spreading peace and enlightenment throughout the galaxy. We've exposed ourselves to too many kinds of solar radiations, too many kinds of localized parasites and diseases."

He held up a hand before his face. The fingers were crusted with gems and filigreed jewels. The fingernails were painted in a variety of patterns and colors. Kane closed the fingers into a broad, hamlike fist. "Strong as we are," he said, "we've been exposed to too many harmful influences. Mutation has crept into the Draconian bloodline. Poison and disease. We need your defensive antibodies, Rogers. We need to breed them into our race. That's going to be your assignment, like it or not. So you might as well like it."

Kane leaned back and stretched languorously. A great yawn escaped him, which he didn't bother to cover. "Besides, if I were you, I think I'd like it a lot!"

"Tell you what, Kane," Buck pointed his finger angrily at the gross figure, "I appreciate your thinking of me, but where I come from we choose our own partners, and the choice means something to us. So—thanks for the offer, but I'll just pass."

"You don't seem to understand, Rogers!" Kane shook his massive head. "You don't have any choice in the matter. You're never going to leave Villus Beta alive, you see?"

"What odds would you like to put on that, Kane?" Buck smiled.

"Gentlemen, gentlemen," Professor Von Norbert broke in. "Can't we all be friends? Here"—he indicated a curtained archway through which a breathtaking young woman emerged, carrying an ornate bowl filled with mouth-watering fruit of both native and imported varieties.

"Let's sit down," Von Norbert went on, "relax, have a bit of refreshment."

The interruption broke the tension that had built between Buck and Kane. Buck followed Von Norbert's suggestion and found a seat for himself, as the professor did likewise. The gorgeous young woman approached Buck and bent to offer him his selection. The filmy, almost transparent clothing that she wore did little to conceal her lush, ripe charms from the earthman as he reached to sample a piece of fruit.

"Try it," the young woman urged him throatily, "I'm sure that you'll really enjoy it."

"Thanks," Buck answered, "don't mind if I do." He lifted a piece of puce-colored fruit shaped like a cross between a mango and a plantain. "You did mean *this*, didn't you?" Buck said.

"I suppose so," the young woman answered. "For now, anyway." She moved away, swaying gracefully with every step.

"There," Von Norbert said to Buck, like a pestered parent trying to soothe a troublesome child, "isn't that better?" He swiveled. "Kane, just let me handle this affair, will you? It's my end of the operation anyway."

Kane heaved his flabby bulk from the throne where he'd been slouched. "All right, Von Norbert. But you'd better have sonny boy cooperating by morning or I'll start using some methods more persuasive than goodies and snacks." He glared at Buck.

Buck met his gaze; as their eyes locked in menace and defiance, Buck spat a large, oval seed on a trajectory that brought it within inches of Kane's shoe. The courtier left angrily and Von Norbert drew his seat nearer to Buck, leaned confidentially toward the earthman.

"Now," Von Norbert said, "I want you to make yourself completely at home here in Villus Beta. We have every facility for your comfort, and I want you to feel free to make full use of those facilities."

"I hate to say this, fella," Buck snapped back, "but I hope you're not counting on all my blood, 'cause I have other plans for it myself."

Von Norbert threw back his head and raised his voice in a high, cackling laugh. "We use the term blood as a metaphor, Captain Rogers. You know, as in bloodlines, blood relations and so on. We do not really want your *blood!*"

Buck's face went white. "You mean—you're after my—ah—my precious bodily fluids?"

"You might say that," Von Norbert grinned. "We are out to breed a generation of humans possessing your antibodies. And only you can be the father of that generation." He turned toward the curtained doorway and smiled at the lush female still standing there, watching Buck Rogers hungrily.

"You will be the father of thousands of sons and daughters, Captain Rogers," the professor reiterated. "Thousands. And all will inherit your immunities."

"Oh, yeah?" Buck challenged. "And how are you going to get me to do it?"

"Perhaps you would like to visit your friend first, for a little conversation," Von Norbert said.

Inside a securely guarded section of Villus Beta, in a row of rooms reserved for special guests, a young woman sat disconsolately before a mirror. The special rooms were furnished comfortably, perhaps even luxuriantly—but they were also as secure as the cells in the heart of a maximum-security block at the archaic prison Alcatraz.

As the door swung open the young woman turned away from the mirror to see who was entering. It was Professor Von Norbert—and, with him, Captain Buck Rogers.

"Buck!" the young woman exclaimed.

"Wilma!" Buck gasped.

The two of them flew to each other's arms. The past friction that had existed between them, the tension that unavoidably occurs when commander and subordinate discover that their official relationship is only one small aspect of the bond between them, disappeared in an instant.

"Buck," Wilma thrilled, "how did you do it? How did you get to me, past so many of them?"

"Uh, I didn't exactly fight my way in, Wilma. In fact, I'm sort of, well, a prisoner here myself."

Wilma drew back from him, her smile fading. "Why are we here? I don't understand. They haven't told me anything. When I ask, they just say, wait."

Buck ventured, "I'm afraid you fell into the trap that they set for me, Wilma. At Rushmore. The shepherds."

Before Wilma could reply, Von Norbert said, "That is precisely so, yes. But," he gestured airily, "it is no problem for us. We have plenty of room here in Villus Beta. And now that you have seen each other, Colonel Deering, Captain Rogers—it is time that we get you along to your, ah, *special* quarters, Captain."

"Don't go, Buck!" Wilma cried. "Watch out for them!"

"That will be enough!" Von Norbert snapped.

"Buck, we'll break out! We have to work together!"

Von Norbert shoved Buck through the doorway, drew it shut behind them with a thump that gave evidence of the heavy security latches built into the structure. Alone inside her room, Wilma Deering slumped onto a seat, her face buried in her hands and her body racked with sobs.

Von Norbert turned Buck over to a squad of burly guardsmen, instructed them to take him to his quarters. "I'll join you shortly," the professor said as Buck was marched away.

As soon as the earthman was out of sight, Von Norbert reached into a pocket, drew out a key and readmitted himself to Wilma's room. The woman shouted past him, using the brief opportunity to get a message to Buck. "Watch out for them," she screamed. "They have drugs that will distort your perception. Be caref . . ."

Her words were cut off as Von Norbert drew an instant pressure-hypo from his pocket, fished it at her. Its chemical freight was in her bloodstream in a fraction of a second. She stopped screaming in the middle of a word and collapsed slowly toward the floor.

Von Norbert caught her. She was not unconscious, just totally relaxed and drained of all will. Norbert carried her toward her bed. She looked up at him smilingly, trustingly, like the young woman who had served the fruit to Buck in Kane's audience chamber.

"That's a good girl," Von Norbert husked into her ear as he put her down gently on the bed. "Just relax and be happy. The Draconians are your friends. I am your friend, Wilma. Remember that. And remember that Buck Rogers is your enemy."

"You're my friend," Wilma repeated dutifully, "Buck Rogers is my enemy."

"That's right," Von Norbert told her. He ran his hand down her cheek, toward her shoulder. "Rogers is your enemy."

He left Wilma, made his way past burly guardsmen and entered Buck Rogers' room. This was a far larger room than Wilma's, set up with a variety of furnishings and decorations to give it a homelike, even folksy atmosphere.

"Well," Von Norbert said, "here is where you will live. Our best accommodations, Captain Rogers."

"Not half bad," Buck commented.

"You must be tired after your long trip."

"Yeah. Pretty beat." Buck yawned. "Think I'll hit the hay."

"Just one more thing, then," Von Norbert said. "A sort of gift for you—a little surprise." He walked to the opposite side of Buck's room, opened a closet door and pulled something from a shelf. It was the computer brain, Theopolis.

"Your compuvisor," Von Norbert said.

Buck's reply was sarcastic: "Super."

"I return it to you as a token of friendship."

"You don't know how good this makes me feel," Buck said.

"Yes, I think I do. Good night, Captain." Von Norbert left, the door giving a heavy, massive *thunk* as he drew it shut.

Buck looked at Theopolis. "All right," he said, "I'm sorry." There was no response. "It was a rotten thing for me to do, trading you away like that." Theopolis still did not reply. "I apologize," Buck said. He waited in vain. "Not talking, huh?"

Despairing of any response from the computer, Buck laid it down and climbed onto the bed. To every outward sign, he was sound asleep within a matter of seconds. As Buck's heavy, steady breathing filled the room, the previously inactive computer flickered once, again, then an array of lights glowed tentatively.

Buck opened one eye, saw the computer blinking on and off. "Caught you," Buck exclaimed.
"Now let's see if you'll talk!"

But Theopolis doused his lights and returned
to dormancy.

"I hope you can talk," Buck said, "because I've
got a plan. And it won't work unless you can talk."
He waited vainly for Theopolis to respond. When
the computer still refused, Buck resumed. "All
right. Don't talk until it's time. But I'm counting
on you to be able to do a good imitation of me.
So you listen carefully, Theopolis!"

Buck whispered his plan to the computer brain.
There was still no reaction. "Okay," he said, "if
it works, it works. If not, Theopolis, I'm going to
make mashed transistors out of you." He crossed
to a high shelf, removed some furnishings from it
and climbed carefully onto its surface. "Okay
now," Buck whispered across the room to Theopolis.

Suddenly Theopolis lit up in full array. He activated his voder circuits and called out in a
perfect imitation of Buck's tones: "Guard! Guard!
Come in here, will ya? How do you work this
thing?"

There was a momentary pause, then the door
swung open and a burly guard strode into the
room. He peered around, looking for Buck Rogers.
"Hey," he demanded, "what's going on in—"

The guard made a single startled grunt as he
took the full weight of Buck's body on his back
and shoulders, as Buck launched himself from the
shelf above the doorway. The guard's laser-pistol
clattered to the floor and skidded halfway across

the room. The guard lunged for it but Buck pulled him back, landed a punch on the side of the guardsman's head.

The guard, a huge man who must have weighed at least half again as much as Buck, hurled his attacker off himself with a snarl. As Buck lunged again, the guard threw himself onto the floor, trying desperately to get hold of his pistol once again. Buck wrestled the guard's hands away from the laser, grappled frantically with the bigger man. The guard landed a piledriver blow to Buck's temple, momentarily stunning Buck while the angry man reached successfully toward the laser.

Before he could bring the pistol into play, his grip on the weapon was challenged by Buck. The two of them grappled on the floor, each striving to point the weapon at the other.

All the while Theopolis lay helplessly watching, blinking his lights on and off frantically, calling words of desperate encouragement to Buck. In the excitement, Theopolis still used Rogers' own voice to give him advice.

The two struggling men staggered to their feet, still locked together in their desperate efforts to control the pistol. It disappeared between their bodies as they clinched. Then there was a flash of blinding light from between them, a small puff of black smoke and a sickening stench of burned cloth and flesh.

The guard fell to the floor and lay unmoving.

Buck Rogers held the laser-pistol in one hand. With the other he lifted Dr. Theopolis, lowered the computer's carrying strap around his neck, and painfully made his way into the hall.

CHAPTER 11.

Wilma Deering lay semi-conscious on the soft bed in her locked room. Her eyes were closed and images flitted through her brain. Recollections of her girlhood in the Inner City of Earth. School days, school friends, girlhood romances, her sensitivity testing and the gasps of admiration and envy from her companions when she was invited to apply for defense squadron flight training.

Her early career, combat missions, training duty, the startling speed of her rise through the ranks.

Her first encounter with Captain Buck Rogers, her overwhelming feelings for him, and—now she had learned of her strange rivalry with the Draconian crown princess Ardala.

Everything, everything. Faces floating before her in mists. Buck. Kane. Dr. Huer. Professor Von Norbert. Draco himself. Ardala. And a voice, a voice whispering in her ear. *I am your friend. The Draconians are your friends. Buck Rogers is your . . . enemy.*

Suddenly someone was shaking her. She opened her eyes. A man was looming above her, his face peering deeply into her own. And, strangely, a flickering, glowing parody of a second face hanging from his neck.

The man was speaking. "Wilma! Wilma! You've got to wake up!"

Wilma raised a hand, brushed a lock of hair away from her face. "Who—what—wait, I can't . . . who is it?"

"It's me," the man said, "Buck."

Suddenly Wilma was wide awake—alarmed and angry. This was the enemy! She leaped to her feet, snarled at him. "Get away from me!"

"Wilma! It's me. Buck."

"I'll kill you if you come any closer," she growled.

"Hey," Buck exclaimed, "snap out of it, I'm your friend."

"You're my enemy," Wilma spat.

"Hey, come on, we gotta get out of here!" He grabbed her to hustle her out of the room—if need be, to carry her. She resisted, and for the second time in as many minutes Buck found himself engaged in a desperate wrestling match.

As they struggled and rolled around the room, Buck managed to gasp at Wilma, "Come on, cut it out, we don't have time to play games. The professor's gonna find us."

"I'll kill you," Wilma reiterated, "the professor is my friend."

Buck broke Wilma's hold on him, tried once more to drag her to her feet and hustle her out of the room. Instead she planted her teeth deep in the muscle of his shoulder. He yelled, jerked away, shot a desperate request to Theopolis: "Hey, what's the matter with Wilma, Theo? Can you take a quick scan on her and figure it out?"

Wilma tried again to get her teeth into Buck. This time he was faced with the need of trying to keep her from escaping and at the same time prevent her from getting her teeth anywhere near his flesh. Dr. Theopolis was pinned between their bodies; his arrays of lights blinked on and off as his scanners analyzed Wilma's condition.

"She seems to be infected with a mind-distorting drug," he gritted. "She must have been brainwashed with the aid of the drug, Buck, so she really believes you're her enemy!"

"Oh, no! You mean she doesn't even *want* to be rescued, Theo!"

"Precisely. You'd better give her a stun-blast from the laser-gun."

Again Wilma broke loose from Buck's grasp. Instead of returning to the attack she sprinted for the door. He dived after her, caught and dragged her back into the center of the room. "And then what?" he asked the computer, "carry her all the way to spaceport on my back, steal a ship and haul her away in it?"

"I think the laser-gun is the only way, Buck."

"There must be something else!"

"There isn't."

"Wait, Theo! I've got it! I'll give Wilma the pistol."

"Buck, that does not compute."

"Oh, no?"

Wilma had continued to struggle with Buck all during his dialogue with Theopolis. She had a hand free now, and used it to grab the laser-pistol that

Buck had previously taken from the guardsman. She leveled the pistol at Buck's chest and commanded him to raise his hands.

Buck complied.

"Now I'm in charge," Wilma asserted.

"It doesn't matter," Buck answered. "Earth has captured Villus Beta, didn't you know that, Wilma? The whole planetoid is in our hands. That pistol can't help you, you might as well surrender."

"I'll never give up," Wilma sneered with an almost Kane-like sound in her voice. "I'll fight to the death."

"Let me go and I'll help you escape to the spaceport," Buck appealed. "I don't know why you've sold out to the Draconians, Wilma, but I'll help you get away if that's what you want."

"You must think I'm stupid, Rogers," Wilma mocked him. "I'm going to Draconia, all right. But I'm taking you with me to stand trial!"

"You'll never make it," Buck told her.

"Just watch me! Now get going. You first, Rogers. I'll be right behind you, with this laser in my hand. One false move and you're zapped— and I won't set it on stun, you can be sure."

Buck meekly exited from Wilma's room, hands in the air, Theopolis hanging around his neck. In the hallway they passed other doors, other crosscorridors. When they reached a major intersection Wilma gestured Buck to halt. She poked her head around the corner, saw a guardsman in full Draconian uniform.

"You earthlings think you can fool me by dressing up your troopers in Draconian uniforms?

Hah!" She stepped around the corner boldly, raised her pistol and zapped the guard.

"I guess we can't fool you," Buck conceded as he stepped over the unmoving form of the guardsman. They continued through the interlocking corridors of the artificial wedge that was the city of Villus Beta, threading their way through a maze until they had reached the giant crossbar that comprised the planetoid's spaceport.

A pair of heavy metallic doors sealed off the port from the rest of the city. Wilma set the laserpistol on a maximum-power needle-beam, cut an opening for them through the doors.

Suddenly two guards shouted a warning from behind them: "Stop, you!"

Slowly Buck turned to face the guards, hands raised in the air. "You win," he surrendered. "Don't shoot." He inclined his head toward Wilma Deering. "She knows, anyway."

"She knows what?" a guard asked.

"It's no use, friend. We can't fool her. She knows we're all earthlings. Our trick fizzled."

The two guards looked at each other in puzzlement. Then one of them addressed Wilma. "Better hand over the weapon, ma'am." He held out his hand for the laser. The other guard moved toward Wilma.

With a lightning movement, Buck knocked aside the gun-arms of the two guards. He couldn't disarm them, could only spoil their aim for a split second. But that was all the time that Wilma needed to squeeze off two quick blasts of her own pistol, sending both guards crumpling to the floor.

Then she looked at Buck, puzzlement in her

face. "What did you do that for?" she asked. "You betrayed your fellow earthmen into my hands."

"I dunno," Buck shrugged. "Just got confused, I guess."

"Well, *I* know what I'm doing anyway," Wilma retorted. "Go on!"

They passed through the double doors into the spaceport. With a shock they realized that it was night on the tiny world—or on this side of it, at least. They had been so long in the artificially controlled environment of the Villus Beta urban area that they had lost all track of night and day.

A fleet of Draconian fighter craft stood at the ready, along with various other types of spacecraft obtained by combat or trade with other planets. Buck's eyes gleamed at the sight of an earthly starfighter of the type used in the defense squadron. His hands itched to take the controls of the rocket.

Through the opening at the end of the spaceport they could see the sky above Villus. Three more planetoids danced in a fantastic saraband, like a triplicated moon, as the tiny worlds made their way in a path around Villus' sun.

Wilma prodded Buck silently with the muzzle of her laser-pistol. She pointed toward the starfighter, urged him with a gesture to move toward the rocket. With a secret smile, Buck complied.

They moved from shadow to shadow across the spaceport. When they halted at last in the shadow of a Citsymian gyrocopter Wilma said, in a low voice, "No tricks now. We'll have to make a run for it, these last few yards. And remember, if those Earth troopers of yours in their phony Draconian

uniforms try to stop us, I'll zap you first and deal
with them later."

Buck nodded. "Here we go," he whispered. He
crouched, ready to make the last sprint to the starfighter, but as he cast a last glance at Wilma he
saw her holding her head in one hand. She staggered once, nearly fell, then lifted her head again
with a startled, somehow puzzled, look on her face.

"What's the matter, Wilma?" Buck asked.

"I don't know," she answered. "I feel so—just
not right." She squeezed her eyes shut, gave her
head a shake as if throwing off an evil spell. When
she opened her eyes again and looked at Buck,
her expression was clear. "But"—she said—"but
you're Buck Rogers. What am I doing?"

"You're getting yourself back together," he
grinned.

Wilma looked down at the laser-pistol she'd
been pointing at Buck. "This is silly," she said.
She slipped the pistol back into her belt. "I'm so
sorry, Buck, I don't know what I was thinking."

"Just what Von Norbert drugged you into thinking," Buck said. "But you had a good time anyhow. Let's get out of here."

They started to sprint across the last few yards
of darkness. They were only feet from the starfighter when night turned into day! The entire
spaceport was suddenly illuminated. Runway
lights, overhead worklamps, landing beams, every
form of light flashed on. Sirens wailed. Trucks and
landcars swarmed over the runways.

And Draconian troops—not squads or even
platoons but whole companies of them, *hundreds*
of grim-visaged, combat-outfitted troops advanced

in solid ranks, converging on the starfighter and the two spotlighted Earth people.

The hatch of the starfighter swung open and a massive, oily-countenanced figure emerged. "Good evening, Rogers. Good evening, Deering," the figure oozed, his voice as thick and smooth as cough syrup. "I've had quite a wait here for you."

"Kane!" Wilma exclaimed.

"At your service, Colonel." The Draconian courtier bowed. "And may I ask what our two star guests were doing at the spaceport?"

"We were out for a midnight stroll," Buck spat bitterly.

"Enjoy the night air," Kane sneered in reply. "It's the last you'll breathe of it for a long time, Rogers. In fact, I'd say for some years—if ever! Your little escapade—which I must say, I anticipated to the last detail—should convince Professor Von Norbert that he'll have to do things *my* way from now on!"

"You mean—no more Mr. Nice Guy, hey, Kane?"

Kane smiled his oiliest smile. "Precisely," he lipped, bowing with ironic exaggeration.

A few hours later, as the weird dawn of Villus Beta sent its eerie light onto the planetoid, Wilma Deering sat disconsolately on the edge of her bed. She could move, but not far—a chain held one ankle to the leg of the bed.

The door ground open and two guards entered, one bearing a metal tray of greasy, unpleasant looking food; the other carrying a primed laser-pistol, ready to fire at a moment's warning. The two guards were followed by the massive form of Kane.

"Breakfast time, Colonel Deering," Kane said cheerily.

Wilma raised tear-reddened eyes to the courtier. "Not hungry, thanks."

"But you must eat," Kane coaxed mockingly, "you have to keep up your strength."

She ignored the tray and Kane's comment equally. "What have you done with Captain Rogers?" she demanded.

"Oh, he's all right. Just undergoing a few routine tests today."

"What routine tests? What are you after?"

"We're after his antibodies. His genetic makeup could strengthen the Draconian race. Or the earthly one, for that matter. But I'm afraid we're going to keep him too busy here for that to have any chance of happening. He's going to father a generation of stormtroopers and fine breeding women for Draconia."

Wilma's mouth dropped. "Is that why you captured Buck? To use him as a—a one-man stud farm?"

"I'm afraid so," Kane chuckled.

Wilma looked down at the metal links that held her to her place. "I suppose you have him chained to a bed too!"

Kane burst into laughter. "Very good, Deering! Don't let us rob you of your sense of humor. Well," he started to move toward the door, "I'll have your guard leave this food here. If you don't find it appetizing while it's fresh and hot, wait till it's sat for a couple of days. We'll let you see Rogers later on—when we're through with him."

He left, followed by the guards.

While Kane was mocking the captive Wilma Deering, Buck Rogers was in Professor Von Norbert's laboratory. For once Kane had told the truth—Von Norbert was running Buck through a series of fitness tests before he embarked on his service in behalf of the Draconian eugenics program.

At the moment Buck was running on a stationary track, its treadmill-like base hooked to a dial that registered total distance run, present speed, average speed, and—via wires connected to monitors taped onto Buck's nearly naked body—such vital data as respiration, blood pressure, and heart action.

"Seven miles in an hour!" Professor Von Norbert exclaimed as he examined a readout indicator. "Superb, Captain Rogers! I'm sure you'll have all the stamina you'll need for our purposes. Well, enough of this!" He reached to a master switch and cut off the moving track.

Buck took a few extra strides. They carried him off the treadmill and he stood on the laboratory floor, facing Von Norbert and catching his breath. "Well, why don't you pull on some clothing while you cool off, and come along with me."

He led Buck past a clothing rack, where the earthman took a superthermal running suit and pulled it on. Then they continued from the lab and into the grand hall where Buck's earlier interview with Kane had taken place.

Kane was again ensconced on the throne. Nearby Wilma stood defiantly between two guards, the chain that had held her to her bed at least temporarily removed. When Buck saw Wilma his grim countenance lighted perceptibly and he managed a low greeting.

Wilma looked at him angrily. "You seem tired," she said bitterly. "I wonder why."

Von Norbert smiled wickedly. "Captain Rogers has had quite a workout, Colonel Deering. I can tell you that his test grades are very high. Most gratifying of all was his mark for—stamina."

"I'll bet it was," Wilma said.

"All right," Kane broke in, "enough social chat. Professor, I want to know—did he meet our requirements?"

"I've wondered about that," Wilma interjected.

"Surpassed them," Von Norbert consulted his clipboard.

Wilma said, "I'll bet!"

"A little more specific," Kane demanded.

"Do I have to be here for this?" Wilma asked.

The others ignored her. Von Norbert consulted his clipboard again. "Seven," he said. "Seven in one hour."

"Excellent," Kane commented.

Wilma stared at Buck, an appraising element added to a combination of wonderment, jealousy, and something close to awe that she felt for him.

CHAPTER 12.

Life on Earth continued as usual. In the endless wilds of Anarchia, of course, no one either knew or cared about the doings of the Inner City. To the wild humans and mutants who roved the rubble-strewn wastes, there was no difference whether Draconia conquered Earth or Earth conquered Draconia; their struggle was the daily one of survival, the life-or-death battle which everyone must eventually lose, but which everyone wants to win first as long as he can.

Within the Inner City, matters were very different. Technicians, food-plant crews, bureaucrats pursued their daily chores. The defense squadron, under the temporary command of Colonel Deering's second-in-command, stood on twenty-four-hour alert, and the normally stringent security rules that applied at the Inner City's Intelligence and Scanning Center had been tripled.

Dr. Huer entered the Intelligence and Scanning Center, striding through security stations as if they didn't exist. He walked up to the chief supervisor and demanded a report.

The supervisor nodded to a senior technician and a star map was thrown upon the main projection screen. "This is where our line-beam scanners lost track of the D-III ship," Latner said. "We're starting to wonder if it merely passed behind a dark sun after all. At this range, we might have been mistaken."

"How?" Huer demanded succinctly.

"We think now," Latner told the savant, "that it might not have been merely a dark star, but a black hole. And the D-III might not have passed behind it, but rather plunged *into* it!"

"And in that case," Huer said, "if the ship re-emerged at all—which it might not have—it could come out in a different portion of the galaxy altogether. Or even in another galaxy!"

"I'm afraid so," Latner conceded. "But we've been calculating possible trajectories, known or suspected re-emergence points for black-hole travel. Of course there's so little experimental data. . ."

"I'm not interested in excuses, Latner!" Huer snapped.

"I'm sorry." The supervisor consulted a computer printout. "Considering the size and weight of a D-III, its speed and trajectory as indicated by Captain Rogers' line-beam at the moment of entry into the hole, our large-scale processing array yielded a set of possible re-emergence vectors in declining order of probability.

"Here," Latner pointed at the screen as a geometric pattern of variously colored lines were superimposed on the star map. "These are the probable vectors remaining after we eliminated those with a probability more than two standard deviations from the max."

"Very well," Huer snapped. "And now what?"

"Next," Latner continued, "we traced the pathways of the remaining course vectors and did a computer-scan comparison of them with known and suspected Draconian presence. Where there was no Draconian presence, we discounted that probability."

Latner waved a hand at the board-tech and the glowing vector lines faded from the screen one by one. Finally only three remained . . . then two . . . finally one.

"Of course, we cannot be absolutely certain," Latner said, "but I can offer you a very high level of confidence, Dr. Huer, that *that*"—and Latner waved a hand forcefully at the map—"will tell us the point of re-emergence and the course followed upon re-emergence by the Draconian D-III!"

Huer shook his head in admiration. "I'd never have thought it of you, Latner," he beamed. "That's the best piece of work the ISC has come up with in months. If not years. How did you ever work that out?"

Latner stood silently, red-faced with embarrassment. Then, after a long pause, the supervisor said, "Actually, Doctor, I didn't work that out. It was, ah, Ellis 14 who did."

Huer turned to the robot armorer. "Well, well, Ellis. And tell me, where did the trace indicate they were headed?"

"Villus Beta, sir," the robot replied. "I'm quite certain that Colonel Deering and Captain Rogers are on Villus Beta. Probably Dr. Theopolis, too!"

Huer nodded thoughtfully. "We'd better scramble a long-range squadron for Villus Beta, then."

He looked at Ellis 14 again, then at Supervisor Latner. "How sure are you of this?"

"Very sure," Ellis 14 said calmly.

"It's our only lead," Latner stated.

"Very well," Huer closed the conversation, "we have no alternative but to try Villus Beta."

Outside the great hall of Villus Beta, a strange quartet strolled through lush gardens, accompanied at a discreet but very safe distance by a squad of tough, ready-for-action Draconian guardsmen. The quartet was made up of two couples: in front, Buck Rogers and Wilma Deering; a few yards behind them, Kane and Professor Von Norbert.

Buck spoke softly, so only Wilma could hear. "Honest, I was just jogging. It was a fitness test, Wilma."

"I don't see what difference it makes to me," the earthwoman snapped.

"That seven in an hour—that was how many miles I could run on a treadmill."

"I really don't care, Captain!"

"Then it won't matter to you. But it's the truth."

Behind them, speaking in an equally low voice so that only his own companion could hear, Von Norbert observed, "They do seem to have an attachment for one another."

"But that doesn't help us create a generation of Draconians with Rogers' antibodies," Kane answered.

"Still, we need to mate him to someone, to be absolutely sure that the antibody chromosome breeds true after five centuries in stasis. We might

as well use the earthwoman as one of our own
females. Rogers will be happier, and we don't
have to use up one of our own specimens for the
final test sequence."

"All right then, Von Norbert, we'll go ahead."
Kane increased his pace so he caught up with
Buck and Wilma within a few strides. They halted
and the four stood confronting one another.

"Buck, Wilma," Kane said in an unusually
friendly tone, "we have formulated a plan. A peace
offering, you might say. We will let the two of you
mate with each other."

Buck and Wilma stared at Kane, then at each
other.

Shortly they were in new quarters—Wilma's
cell-like room and Buck's more homespun surroundings had both been cleared for other uses,
and the two Earth people were alone in a specially
prepared setting. It was a fine example of the
Betan penchant for combining indoor and outdoor
elements in the same setting.

There were ferns, moss, and exotic succulents
growing, and a stream wandered through the
room, coming to a miniature waterfall that
splashed into a glistening pond. Music wafted
through the air, coming from unseen speakers, and
perfumes floated on warm breezes. There were
platters of tempting foods, pitchers of wine, even
the occasional flash of silver as a fish leaped in the
pond below the waterfall, or the flapping of a
fantastically colored bird overhead.

Buck and Wilma stood flabbergasted until they
heard the door slam shut behind them. It was like

being locked into the Garden of Eden. Who would
want to leave?

Hand in hand they wandered through the artificial paradise. Buck stopped beside a bowl of
fruit, examined several of the tempting items it
contained, and remarked, "They're very big on
fruit around here." He took a bite of a sort of
plum-papaya, commented favorably on its flavor
and poured two glasses of wine. "Say, this stuff
is really fine. Have a glass."

"Better go slow," Wilma replied. "This might
be drugged."

A look of alarm appeared on Buck's face. He put
down the glasses of wine. "Well, let's try something else."

He found a sylvan bower, tested it with his
fingertip and grinned. "Hey, Wilma, dig this!"

She came over and knelt beside him. "Well I'll
be," she exclaimed, "a concealed vibra-aqua-mat-
tress floating bed." She prodded the seeming
ground around the edges of the moss-simulating
mattress, found a toggle switch, and clicked it to
a new position.

Directly over the floating bed an image screen
glowed into being. "Look at this, Buck. You either
have to be lying in the bed, or somehow crouch
with your head turned around a hundred-eighty
degrees to see the show. But it's pretty good!"

Buck gazed at the screen. It showed a couple in
amorous embrace. The image was fully dimen-
sional, in full color, and with super-quad sound.
Buck watched for a few seconds, started to blush
at what he saw on the screen, and reached for the
toggle switch. He cut off the projection.

"Boy, that stuff gets everywhere," he said.

Wilma smiled. "You *are* such a gentleman, Buck Rogers. In your own crummy way!"

"My mama always said I shoulda been a truck driver. Huh! I guess she was right after all. What's the difference between that and a rock-jock, anyhow? At least they had roads to follow and rest-stops every couple of hundred miles."

"Don't be so downcast," Wilma sympathized. She took his hands. "You're really very . . . likable, Buck."

He smiled nervously. "You too," he managed to blurt.

They took a step toward each other, halted. Buck slid his hands around Wilma's slim, supple waist and drew her closer to him. She did not resist, but rather moved willingly toward him until their bodies brushed, with only the thin layers of Draconian-supplied cloth separating them.

For a moment they gazed into each other's eyes. Their mouths met, and then—Buck pulled away. "We can't," he said bitterly, "not here."

Wilma's face showed surprise and disappointment. "What's the difference?"

"I don't know," Buck shook his head. "I just know there's something fishy going on here. We both know what a scoundrel Kane is, and as for Von Norbert, I wouldn't trust that high-and-mighty professor any farther than I could throw a D-IV super-spaceliner."

"So—what does that have to do with us?" Wilma gestured with one hand, indicating their beautiful surroundings as well as themselves.

"Just that—if they're making it so easy for us

to get together . . . setting up this little Eden for us, providing a cozy little love nest in the middle of it, even furnishing us with free 3Vs to give us the idea if we didn't have it ourselves . . . then Kane and Von Norbert must have some sort of motive of their own that I just don't trust. I don't know what it is, but if it's good for the enemy it's pretty sure to be bad for us."

Wilma slumped disconsolately into a crouch. "You're right."

"On the other hand," Buck knelt on the mossy ground beside her and slid an arm around her shoulders, "if this is what we both want anyway . . ."

They clung together for a long, tender embrace. This time it was Wilma who pushed Buck away from her. "I'm sorry, Buck," she said. There were tears in her eyes. "But I keep thinking—what if you were right? I mean—before—what if we're just playing into their hands by . . . this . . ."

"Yeah," Buck grunted. He heaved himself to his feet and walked away from Wilma. "Why did I have to think of that, just when everything was so nice?"

With tears now falling from Wilma's eyes, and Buck's expression no cheerier than Wilma's, they remained, yards from each other, backs turned to one another, while a grim silence descended upon them both. Through it they could hear the tinkling of the little stream, the steady purring sound of the miniature waterfall, the occasional cry of a bird or splash of a fish.

"What fun," Buck grumbled miserably.

A few hours later, Buck lay stretched on the yielding moss, staring at a swaying fern. Soft music played. For all his strength and stamina, and for all the emotional tension of the situation, he finally yielded to sleep. As his breathing became deep, steady, rhythmic, Wilma Deering trod slowly and softly across the open area between them.

She knelt beside the sleeping man, touched his face with her trembling fingertips. He started to stir. Wilma drew back, held her breath. Buck subsided into unconsciousness again. Wilma sighed, rose to her feet, walked away.

Buck awoke, found the lighting low, the music soft in the miniature Eden. He looked through the gloom, saw Wilma sitting miserably with her back to him, staring abstractedly at nothing.

Buck walked to a bowl of fruit, selected a juicy melonito, started toward Wilma as if to offer it to her as an opening conversational gambit. He halted behind her, aware that she sensed his presence and chose to avoid any exchange.

He walked back to the bowl and dropped the melonito into it again. "Damn it," he grumbled, "this place has everything we need but a cold shower."

Still later, Buck and Wilma sat face to face. They had improvised a gaming circle on the ground of their Eden. From two bunches of grapes, one vividly verdant, the other lushly purple, they had improvised a batch of marbles. They shifted their positions, knelt opposite each other, just beyond the boundaries of the circle, in the time-honored fashion of marble-shooters.

"Okay," Buck was explaining. "I'm sorry that this great old game has somehow died out. Maybe we can reintroduce it to Earth if we ever make it back there from Villus.

"Now, all the marbles are divided into regular marbles and shooters. Here"—he reached toward a nearby bowl of fruit—"this plum is going to be my shooter. Now, the object of the game is to knock your opponent's marbles out of the circle. You use your shooter to . . ."

In the great hall of Villus Beta, Professor Von Norbert stood beside Kane, watching the proceedings in Buck and Wilma's Eden with angry and disappointed expressions.

"So much for your methods of subtle persuasion," Kane growled. He reached with one hand and flicked off the telescreen on which they had been watching the Earth people. The concealed monitor-camera that had been focused on Buck and Wilma continued to scan their activities, but Kane and Von Norbert no longer watched.

Von Norbert shook his head. "I can't understand it. Everything was carefully calculated—the setting, the music, the soft perfumes with the aphrodisiac gases blended into them. How could I fail?"

"*Argh*, that's what you intellectuals always wind up wondering," Kane gritted. "Call me barbarian if you want to, but for my scrip it's the iron fist that does the job. If anybody gets in your way, don't reason with him. *Smash him!* They learn soon enough to obey."

"You may be right," Von Norbert conceded. "But with the Princess Ardala arriving in a few hours, what are we going to have to report to Her Highness?"

"That's your problem, Von Norbert. I handle the military side of things, and I've been doing a damned fine job, if I say so myself. If you can't handle your job, you might want to try out for another one—like, a member of the stoker gang! Ah, ha-ha-ha-ha-ha!"

CHAPTER 13.

Kane and Professor Von Norbert stood side by
side once again. This time it was for the formal
welcome of the Princess Ardala to Villus Beta. The
spaceport was spic-and-span. Draconian troops
were ranged in precise formation, their uniforms
clean and pressed, the metal accouterments of the
equipment polished to a blinding brightness in the
ever-changing light of the Villus star-complex.

A Draconian military band played the harsh and
strident airs of the official Draconian military rep-
ertoire—music marked by strident brasses and loud
percussion, music that raised the hackles and set
the blood to pounding, music designed to rouse
and anger the hearer.

The spaceship that hove into view was of the
largest class ever constructed. Of Draconian design, it would have made a magnificent spaceliner
for the passenger run or the cruise trade; or, con-
verted for freight, it could have carried uncounted
metric tons of agricultural products, industrial raw
materials, or useful manufactured goods between
the stars.

But being of Draconian design, the D-VIII was
furnished as a battlewagon. It bristled with laser-

howitzers, space-torpedo launching tubes, space-marine assault-craft bays, heavy-bomber launching decks, armories and fuel and ammunition dumps.

The only compromise on the D-VIII was the Imperial Suite. Outfitted now for the use of the Princess Ardala, the suite had every sensuous luxury imaginable to the mind of twenty-fifth century designers. There was hardly a world in the Draconian Empire that had not been looted to yield up some fillip of comfort and self-indulgence for the princess.

As the D-VIII settled with military precision into the receiving pods of the Villus Beta spaceport, the battlewagon's repellor beams dancing in multicolored patterns beneath her hull, the band struck up a strident, military air.

As the main passenger hatch swung open and the princess emerged, along with her personal entourage of sycophants and retainers, the band swung into the Draconian Imperial Anthem, a tune—if its angry, discordant tones could be said to make up a tune—reserved for personal appearances by the Emperor Draco and members of the immediate imperial household alone.

The princess was garbed in flowing satin robes trimmed in barbaric natural furs. Her breathtaking, vaguely exotic features were framed by a mass of rippling, blue-black hair as thick and as beautiful as the coat of a wild Yuggothian ice-otter. She sneered at the military band and tossed a glittering coin at the feet of its conductor, swept past the musicians, ignored battalions of smartly saluting soldiers, strode up to Kane and Von Norbert and accepted her official welcome.

"My dear Princess Ardala," Kane hissed, "welcome to our little outpost here in the boonies."

The princess' eyes snapped. "It's most charming, Kane, for a backwoods rustic village. All that mars its rural perfection is your presence."

She sneered at the fawning Kane, turned a chilling smile upon Professor Von Norbert. "And your side of things?" Ardala demanded.

"I, also, welcome you to Villus Beta, Your Imperial Highness," the scientist bowed formally.

"Hah! I've had enough of ceremony and abasement, Von Norbert. I want to see the results of your experiments. The empire needs results, and you'd better have something good to show me!"

"Yes, Your Royal Highness. If you wish to be briefed immediately, we can cover the situation on the way to my laboratory."

Ardala indicated assent with an imperious gesture. They started to walk, the professor explaining the theories of his work in layman's terms as they moved past saluting soldiers. By the time they reached the edge of the spaceport he had moved on to the experimental aspect of his project. Ardala's questioning was probing and ruthless.

When she uncovered the information that Von Norbert had been unable to maneuver Buck Rogers into mating with Wilma Deering, Ardala burst into vicious, spiteful laughter. "I know that Colonel Deering of Rogers'," she snarled. "For once the man shows a little discernment."

"But, Your Highness," Von Norbert countered, "you see that Rogers' recalcitrance has stymied the experimental side of my work. The theory is completely developed, up to this point. But we must have experimental verification in order to move on to the practical application of my theories."

Kane had been pacing angrily along with the other two, listening in silence to their discussion of Von Norbert's work. Now Kane put in, "Whatever you do, Ardala, I don't want you to trust that Rogers!"

"Thank you, Kane," the princess snapped. "When my imperial father appointed you my guardian, however, he failed to notify me of the act, so I think I shall go on ignoring your worthless opinions as I have done in the past."

"Ah, to return to a scientific topic," Von Norbert interrupted timidly, "I'm afraid that if we can't convince Rogers to help us, we are without his antibodies. You can't just order a man to . . . to . . . procreate."

Ardala smiled, almost for the first time since her arrival aboard the imperial D-VIII battlewagon. "It depends on who his partner is, Professor. For instance, if I were to. . ."

"Hah, but you aren't!" Kane sneered. "The computer did the choosing, Ardala, and even if you were willing, it didn't pick you!"

"Moreover," the professor interjected, aghast, "the imperial princess, the heiress-apparent to the throne of Draco himself . . . !"

"A princess, yes," Ardala hissed. "But first, I am a woman. Remember that. Well—all things in the name of science, eh? Come along. In any case, I want to see Captain Rogers."

"And Wilma Deering?" Kane asked.

"Not particularly," Ardala replied. "But if you're keeping them penned together, however unsuccessfully, I suppose I must."

While Kane escorted Ardala to a lush garden near the professor's laboratory, Von Norbert went ahead and brought Buck and Wilma back with him, accompanied by armed guards to prevent their escape. Kane briefed Ardala on progress within the Villus sector of space while they waited for the others.

When Buck and Wilma arrived, Buck bowed before the Princess Ardala. His movements and posture had all the proper forms dictated by imperial court etiquette—but his expression was one of mockery rather than respect.

Wilma and Ardala ignored each other's presence completely.

Buck rose from his bow before the princess. "Ardala," he said, dropping court formalities, "how nice of you to drop in."

"How nice of you to be here when I arrived." Ardala's voice dripped rancid honey.

"Thank you," Buck acknowledged. "Actually, it wasn't exactly my idea. Your friend Kane here had a little to do with it."

"Kane is no friend of mine," Ardala shot back. "The man is an obvious social climber and power seeker. If I weren't heiress to Draco's throne, Kane wouldn't give me a second glance."

"That isn't true!" Kane blurted angrily. "I would, too—"

"Are you calling the Princess Ardala a liar?" Ardala interrupted Kane, referring to herself in deliberately formal terms.

"No, no, of course I wouldn't insult Your Royal Highness," Kane backed away from his denial.

"Then you admit it," Ardala triumphed, "you are nothing but a social-climbing power-seeker. Well, Kane, since you admit your own perfidy—"

"But—" Kane spluttered, "but—but. . ." His face turned beet red beneath his disorderly, greasy, black locks. "Oh, I give up, Princess. Have it any way your warped imagination would have it. But don't think your father won't hear about this!"

Ardala gave forth peal after peal of shrill, mocking laughter. When she finally regained her composure she said, "My father, the Emperor Draco, is off commanding his fleet against the Gregorians. He left me in complete charge of operations at home. Do you wish to file a formal protest of my conduct? With me?" she grinned wickedly.

Kane threw his arms out in disgust. Ardala did not so much intimidate him as enrage him with her behavior.

"Well, then." The princess turned back toward Captain Rogers. "Now then, Buck, what are we going to do with you?" she asked.

"I have a great idea," Buck said, "just send me home. Me and Wilma, that is—and our friend Theopolis while you're at it."

"I have a better idea," Ardala said. "Wilma and that stupid box of flashlight bulbs can go home. I'll even furnish them with a ship and an escort. You stay here."

"Nope," Buck shook his head. "Good, but not good enough."

"Oh, all right," Ardala said sweetly. "Obviously

Wilma is causing the difficulty, so if you won't let me send her home I'll just have the guards kill her. Right here and now.

"Guards!" She gestured commandingly.

"Here," Ardala said, "take this woman away and kill her. Don't take too long about it, but don't hurry too much. I want you to enjoy yourselves thoroughly before she's all used up."

The guards seized Wilma and prepared to hustle her away.

"Uh, wait a minute," Buck said. "Come to think of it, Princess, I might reconsider your first offer."

"Now you're cooking with gas, Rogers. As some of Von Norbert's twentieth-century forebears might have said." She turned. "Guards, release her. But don't go away, hey?"

"You can do anything you want to with me," Wilma snapped at her rival. "You'll never get either Buck or me to do anything for you. We'll never collaborate with Draconia against Earth!"

Buck turned to face Wilma. "Wait," he urged. "Let's at least hear what Ardala has to say."

"Buck!" Wilma exclaimed in shock.

"Hey," he said. "The lady flew thousands of light years through hyper-null space just to come and see us. The least we can do is hear what she wants to say to us. There's no harm in listening, Wilma."

"Buck, I never thought you'd commit treason!" She started to stomp away in anger. Her guards shot an inquiring look at Ardala, to see whether they were to stop Wilma from departing. Instead, at Ardala's gesture, they accompanied the earthwoman as she strode to the opposite end of the garden and stood pouting.

"How convenient," Ardala commented. She smiled and drew a breath. "Now, Buck, I'll be honest with you."

"Really?" he asked in astonishment.

Ardala ignored the jibe. "The Draconian race is dying out," she said. "We're slowly being decimated by diseases. Simple little diseases that were of no consequence in your day because people had antibodies to fight them with. You have those antibodies, too, Buck. They were bred into the chromosomes of the human race. But in the past five hundred years they've disappeared. Only you still have them. That's why we need your help.

"Buck," she stood very close to him—*very* close to him. She was almost the same height as he, and their faces nearly touched as she spoke. "If you'll do us this one favor, we'll do anything we can in return. Aaaan-y-thiiiing," she said slowly.

Buck remained silent for thirty seconds, carefully considering the reply he would make—and, also, carefully timing the moment of maximum impact. Too quick an answer would not be so effective as one led up to by a dramatic pause— but if he waited too long, Ardala's tension would peak and begin to subside again.

"Will you let me know everything," Buck asked finally, "that your genealogical computers can turn up concerning my family?"

Ardala decided that she was getting off with astonishing ease. "Absolutely," she said.

"All right," Buck gestured toward the path leading out of the garden. "Let's go."

"Wait a minute," Kane put in. "How do we know this earthworm will keep his word, Ardala? We have nothing to make us believe in his good faith."

"I've got to admit you're right, Kane. For once in your life."

Kane faced Buck Rogers, chuckling in triumph. "All in good time, me Buck-o. Once we *know* you're serious about helping us. *Then* we can see about satisfying your curiosity."

"Provided there's a mutual pledge," Buck agreed. "Ardala, we have our disagreements, but I believe you'll keep your word about this. But there's another condition. I want you to sign a non-aggression treaty with the Inner City."

Kane roared with laughter. "Are you joking, Rogers? Don't you remember—Draconia was ready to sign a treaty with the Inner City and *you* meddled with the negotiations and botched the whole deal!"

"That was a false treaty, Kane. A cover story for a treacherous invasion, as you well know. I mean an *honest* treaty, with full provisions for enforcement and inspection."

"Never," the burly Kane snarled.

"Agreed," Ardala overruled him, provoking a glare of pure hatred from the oily Kane.

"And the first thing you do, to show your good faith—since you're the ones who first raised that question—is to send Wilma back to Earth. In the Earth ship standing on the Villus Beta landing field right now!"

A slow smile crept across Ardala's face, the very opposite of the glare that radiated angrily from

Kane's. Things were working out precisely as the princess would have hoped that they would—and not at all as Kane would have preferred.

Of course, when Wilma Deering heard of the deal that had been struck between Buck Rogers and Princess Ardala, behind Wilma's back, she was less than delighted. In fact, by the time she reached the spaceport to board the rocket for Earth, she was kicking, screaming, biting, and altogether being carried and dragged more than she was walking to the ship. After a struggle the Draconian guards had her loaded into the ship and locked into its cabin. But as the commander of the detachment commented when he reported to Ardala on the completion of his task, "She is in the ship, Your Royal Highness. But—how can we make her fly it to Earth? And if she refuses, what becomes of your bargain with Captain Rogers?"

"I'll take care of that, officer," Buck Rogers said. "If you agree, Ardala—I'll go and have a talk with Wilma."

"In a spaceship, fully fueled and ready to blast off?" the princess asked incredulously.

"I give you my word," Buck stated, "I will return here as soon as I've talked with Wilma. Whatever the outcome of our discussion."

The princess sighed. "Very well, Buck. I may be a fool, but . . ." She waved him toward the ship.

As soon as Buck clambered into the rocket ship's cabin, Wilma Deering tore into him with an attack of verbal viciousness that exceeded anything she had ever said to him before. "You are nothing but a traitor, Buck Rogers!" she screamed.

"Giving in to their demands! Buck! How can

you believe that sappy story about saving their
race? And why should you help save them anyway? They're the enemy of Earth!"

"Will you calm down, Wilma?" Buck tried to
soothe her by patting her hand with his own, but
she pulled angrily away from him. He tried with
words again: "What have you to gain by staying
here?" he asked. "They'll kill you, Wilma. They
don't need you—just me. So you're their trump
card against me! If I get out of line, they torture
you. Threaten your life, even. I can't live with that.
You got your choice, lady—you can stay here and
wind up tortured to death, or you can fly back to
Earth in this ship, and be free."

"But I don't want to be free!" Wilma sobbed.
"I want to protect my planet from these vicious
fiends."

"They're not so bad," Buck temporized.

"You're saying that just because that woman
has the hots for you!"

"Don't be silly, Wilma! I just want us both to
play the best odds we can get. You go back to
Earth and tell them where I am. You can lead a
rescue fleet back here to Villus Beta."

Wilma thought about that for a long time. Finally she said, half-questioningly, "I can r-rescue
you?"

"Yes," Buck affirmed. "That's why I want you
to go." Still she hesitated, and he leaned forward
and kissed her gently.

"All right," Wilma agreed.

The Princess Ardala watched the takeoff of
Wilma's starfighter with deeply satisfied eyes. As

the ship disappeared into the black void above Villus Beta, the princess turned to the man at her side and asked a question.

"Exactly whom do you plan to have Rogers mate with, Professor?"

"I'll show you, Your Highness," Von Norbert replied. He led the princess from the spaceport to the nearby great hall, where she unhesitatingly took the seat of the ruler. "All right, Professor, now let's see your show."

Von Norbert gave a signal, and three young women traipsed into the hall from behind a row of shimmering, gossamer curtains. One of them had green hair and eyes, and smooth, creamy skin with a distinctly greenish cast to it. The second was similarly colored in blue—blue hair, blue eyes, beautiful pale blue skin. The final young woman was orange: orange of hair, orange of eye, orange of skin.

Each of the three was more than beautiful: each was absolutely spectacular. Their figures would have astonished the most rabid of spaceborne pin-up collectors. Their costumes were suggestive of spacesuits, but instead of protecting the bodies from the ravishes of vacuum and radiation, they exposed all to the devouring eyes of any interested observer.

"Here they are, my princess," Von Norbert announced proudly. "Three of the loveliest creatures in the known universe. Grenda . . . Blorim . . . and Orell. Selected by computer with the primary desideratum their physical charms, of course—but also with points assigned to stamina, intellect, and esprit de corps."

The Princess Ardala inspected Grenda, Blorim, and Orell closely, paying no more attention to them as persons than a stockbreeder does in inspecting a herd of cattle. After she had examined all three with an almost microscopic thoroughness, she turned to Von Norbert and said, "Not good enough!"

"But—but they're the *best*, Your Highness!" Von Norbert stammered. "Perfect for our needs. Look —just look at those pelvic regions!" He seized a pointer and prodded one of the young women on display. "Perfect for mothering the next generation!"

"They are not good enough . . . for Buck Rogers," Ardala reiterated. "The man deserves the very best. He deserves—a princess!"

Kane smashed one mighty fist onto the polished wooden surface of a gorgeously crafted table, splintering the table into little more than sawdust. "That does it!" he shrieked. "I'm calling your father, the emperor! He'll return from the battlefront when he hears of this insolence!"

Ardala smiled and stroked Kane's bristling cheek with a set of long, graceful, barbarously painted fingernails. "You're just being jealous, Kane. But I wouldn't marry you anyway, even if I hadn't found Buck. I'm just not interested in your bungling pomposity."

Kane roared an obscenity and stamped furiously from the hall.

Professor Von Norbert smiled grimly. "I don't wish to offend Her Highness," he addressed Ardala. "But we *are* conducting a military experiment. The war with the Gregorians is not going

well, and its outcome hangs in the balance. If
we can't produce a new crop of soldiers with full
immunities within the next five years at most, we
will have to give up our hopes of conquering the
Gregorian system.

"Your Highness," he went on obsequiously,
"much as I tremble to interfere with the princess'
personal life, I must submit that we cannot let
anyone's romantic ambitions interfere with our
work."

"So," Ardala replied hotly, "now you're turning
on me, too, Von Norbert? After my personally
funding your experiments? Hah! You talk about
war. I'm talking about love! *I want Buck Rogers!*"

Professor Von Norbert ran his hand through his
thinning gray hair. He had an air of youthful energy about him most of the time, but now he
looked, suddenly, far older than usual. "Princess
Ardala," he said, "I'm your friend. I'm a friend of
your father the emperor. I used to bounce you on
my knee when you were a baby. In fact, I bounced
all of the thirty royal daughters on my knee when
they were babies."

"Yes, yes," Ardala seethed.

"I've known you all your life," Von Norbert continued. "I would do nothing to harm you. But—"

"I knew a *but* was coming," Ardala complained.
"All of that dear old Uncle Von Norbert business
had to be a buildup for something. So—what is it,
dear old Uncle Von Norbert?"

"We must go by the will of computer," the
professor supplied. "If it says you make an accept-
able mate for Buck Rogers . . . and if that is

what the royal will desires, of course . . . then
you may mate with him."

"Good," Ardala said. "The computer won't dare
deny my wishes!"

"We shall see what the readout says," Von Norbert answered neutrally. "Plus, of course, Captain
Rogers' other mates. There must be hundreds of
them. Thousands, in fact. In fact . . ."

Ardala cut him off again. "You listen to me, you
professorial nincompoop! I am a princess. I am
one princess, alone, the last remaining of the emperor's daughters who has not married herself to
some simpering weakling. If I have to share Buck
Rogers with thousands of brood-cows just to conquer the Gregorian system, then we can cancel
our conquest of the Gregorian system. Draconia
owns hundreds of solar systems, all across the
galaxy. Thousands of them! Who needs one more?"

"We are bound by the computer, Your Highness," Von Norbert said. He began to escort the
princess to the Villus Beta computer center. She
swept before him with regal hauteur.

The Betan computer center was designed with
full attention to the requirements of the machines,
and only passing consideration for the needs of
their users. Giant panels of circuit modules and
indicator diodes filled vast volumes of space, while
power supply systems, environmental stabilizers,
titanic heat-sinks and high-capacity storage devices extended the size of the center to imposing
degrees.

In the very innermost location of the computer
center Professor Von Norbert and Princess Ardala
halted. Here, in a sparkling, antiseptic room de-

void of any sign of human life, a master inquiry-board and communications module stood. It was fitted with keyboard, printer, telescreen, voder, and audio-input circuits, pattern recognition readers, and every other conceivable form of equipment usable for communication with a computer.

"Well," Von Norbert announced proudly, "here it is! The most advanced computing facility in the entire Draconian realm—probably, in the entire known galaxy!"

"Good," Ardala commented. "Get out!"

Von Norbert was stunned. "I beg Your Highness' pardon. Did I hear Your Highness say—"

"You bet your britches you heard me. Scram, Professor!"

"But—but, Your Highness!" He was nearly in tears.

"Listen here, dear old Uncle Von Norbert. Can this computer understand what I say to it?"

"But of course," Von Norbert said. His confidence was beginning to return, now that he was back on technical ground. "You may activate a microphone and speak to it, type your message by keyboard, write it on the sensaplate with stylus, tap it in by telegrapher's code. . . ."

"Fine," Ardala stopped him again. "Voice will do fine. Well, and maybe I'll play around with some of the other toys you have on here. So this is what you do with the money I get you out of the imperial treasury. Build yourself shiny toys!"

"Your Highness!"

"Scram!"

Von Norbert bowed out with quivering chin. Ardala sat at the computer's console, tapped a few symbols via keyboard, then flicked an input mode control switch to *oral*.

The computer spoke in its electronically synthesized voice. "Villus Compu at your service."

"Good," Ardala said, "do you recognize me? Here's my handprint, check it with your files."

"You are Princess Ardala, twenty-sixth daughter of Draco, king of Draconia and emperor of the Draconian realm."

"That's right, you old bag of diodes and chips. I am also beautiful, intelligent, and very loving. And I desire to mate with Captain Buck Rogers of Terra."

"Negative," the computer voiced, "your personality scan is not appropriate for this experiment."

"What are you talking about? You're nothing but a machine! You don't just say *negative* to me—I'm a princess! I *order* you to have Buck Rogers mate with me!"

"Negative. Your personality scan indicates independent, hard to get along with, apt to rant and rave. This experiment is for the breeding of soldiers, who must be subject to discipline and conformity. You are not suitable."

"What do you mean?" Ardala ranted. "I've never ranted or raved in my life!" she screamed. "Where's something heavy? Give me. . ."

She ran around the room, searching. Finally she opened the top of the console keyboard unit and pulled out a heavy paper roller. She was about to smash the computer's visiscreen when it sprang to life with the image of her father.

The Emperor Draco, it should be understood, has been criticized for his ambition, his ruthless-

ness, his vicious temper, his gourmandlike appe-
tite for all fleshly pleasures including food, drink,
lush women, fast vehicles, vainglory, palaces, vil-
las, high-speed groundcars, yachts, and spaceships.
In fact, all of this criticism is entirely valid—and
then some.

But Draco was also brilliantly intelligent, vastly
skilled at both political and military sciences, absolutely fearless, and—in his own, brutal way—
fiercely loving and loyal to all of his daughters
and all of his empire.

Huge, bearded, garbed in the uniform of stellar
high admiral—which title he bore in addition to
his royal and imperial ones, and which he had
earned by dint of sheer military brilliance quite
aside from his position on the throne—Draco
peered out of the computer screen and commanded his daughter.

"Ardala! Put that down at once!"

The furious princess of a moment before turned
into a naughty child, discovered and scolded by
a righteous, stern parent. She fumblingly installed
the paper roller back into the keyboard. "Yes,
Father," she said contritely.

"Daughter," Draco's visage intoned, "I am very
upset, very disappointed with you. Here I am
having the time of my life in the middle of a perfectly glorious space war. Thousands of ships. Millions of troopers. Casualties all over the place.
Blood, gore, screams of the wounded, moans of
the dying, etc., etc. And I just received the most
distressing summons away from my duties."

"Don't listen to Kane," Ardala pleaded. "You
know he's just jealous. He wants to marry me and

be a prince, and I spurned him and he's mad. I love you, Daddy."

"Now you listen to me, young lady. This Gregorian war is no trifling matter. We are determined to conquer the Gregorians. We must win. *I* must win! And if you do anything to interfere with my victory, I will have you executed as a traitor."

"But, Daddy," Ardala sniffled.

"No buts! Do you understand?"

"Yes, Daddy," Ardala sobbed.

CHAPTER 14.

The Ellis Plan was what they called it, in honor of the robot armorer Ellis 14 who had worked out the logical procedure involved. Supervisor Latner had fumed and protested but the old scientist Dr. Huer had insisted, and the Ellis Plan it was.

When it went into effect, the Inner City defense squadron ready detachment was cut back to skeleton level, with all duty crews on twenty-four-hour alert, while a special force was sent at top speed, star-warp drive, to trace the vector calculated in the Intelligence and Scanning Center.

The point ship of the special expeditionary force was piloted by Wilma Deering's deputy commander and executive officer, Major Dylan. Dylan's screen was set for a maximum range scan, and the pilot's keen eyes seldom strayed from the eerily glowing rectangle. Suddenly Dylan's eyes widened. A blip!

It was too remote, or too small, an object—or one both too remote *and* too small to register on the range-and-mass indicator in Dylan's starfighter, but it was an object in a sector of space where no objects were normally to be found. And it was moving as fast as only a starfighter in star-warp drive could move—directly toward the defense squadron!

"Ship in twelfth quadrant," Dylan snapped into the starfighter's radiophone, "identify yourself."

There was a brief pause filled with only the space-crackle of free-floating hydrogen nuclei colliding in random combinations. Then a familiar voice spoke through Dylan's earphones: "This is Colonel Deering, Inner City, earth space fleet. Request ID data on yourself!"

With a grin of relief the exec radio'd back, "Colonel Deering! This is your fleet! Dylan speaking—I'm in temporary command for this sector!"

"Oh, it's so good to hear you!" Relief was clear in Wilma's voice.

"Are you all right?" Dylan asked.

"Yes. Fine."

"And Captain Rogers?"

"He's—he's still on Villus Beta," Wilma told the other pilot. "He helped me escape so I could return to Earth for help."

"Well, you don't have to go that far. Help's here now! Are you ready to assume command of the squadron, Colonel, or shall I continue to act for you?"

Wilma drew a deep breath. "Yes," she said, "thank you, Dylan, for acting in my absence. And for bringing help this far. I'll resume command now, thanks again."

She swung the controls of her starfighter around, warped her flight path to match that of the speeding fleet. She saw Dylan's ship, on her screen, falling back to exec position, leaving the command position open for her. With a joyful heart, Wilma

swung her starfighter into formation with the rest
of her command and rocketed onward with the
others.

On Villus Beta, Buck Rogers and Professor Von
Norbert had left their respective interests and
were—to put it delicately—negotiating terms.
They stood in the room that had first been assigned to Buck for housing, before he and Wilma
had experienced their abortive romance in the
artificial Garden of Eden.

The two men had apparently reached some level
of understanding, as Buck's words at the moment
were, "All right. I'll do it, Professor.

"But"—he went on—"no more cozy mating
room. And especially no more public perfor-
mances!"

"Why—what do you mean?" Von Norbert asked
innocently.

"This!" Buck snapped. He pried away a ventilator grating to reveal a sleek video monitor lead.

Von Norbert said, "Oh."

"Well?" Buck persisted.

"That wasn't for public performance. It's a routine security monitor. They're all over Villus Beta.
I've found 'em in my own quarters. Nobody's quite
sure who controls them. Probably Kane."

"Well, I want my room cleaned of the things.
No bugs—or no Buck! If you understand what I'm
saying."

"All right," Von Norbert agreed, "I'll have your
room completely debugged. You can check it yourself as soon as the squad leaves."

"Then it's okay," Buck said, "I suppose."

"All right. While the security troops are clearing out their equipment, let's stroll over to the great hall and meet some of your, ah, counterparts in the experiment." The professor led the way from Buck's quarters.

In the great hall Buck was introduced to Grenda, Blorim, and Orell. They all cooed hellos at Buck. He offered to shake hands politely with each, discovered that they were willing to do far more than shake hands with him.

"Well," Buck commented, "this is a pleasure." Orell snuggled up to Buck on one side; Blorim, on the other; Grenda stood against his chest, looked up and stroked his cheek. "This is more than a pleasure, in fact," Buck conceded.

"Uh," he stammered, "ah, Grenda. Uh, Grenda. Uh, what kind of name is that?"

"Draconian, silly," the voluptuous young woman replied.

"Oh," Buck commented intelligently. He turned to one side. "And, uh, Blorim. Blorim. That's Draconian too?"

"Of course," the second young woman answered. "Of course."

The third young woman, Orell, asked, "What kind of name is Buck?"

"American, silly," the earthman told her.

"What's that? American, I mean."

"Oh," Buck explained, "it's a country. Or—it used to be."

"Bet you can't guess how old we are, Buck," Blorim teased.

The professor interjected a stern word.

"Whoops! Sorry," the young woman responded.

"No. I hadn't thought to ask. How old are you?" Buck asked.

Blorim shot an inquiring glance at the professor. In reply he merely shook his head.

"I hear that *you're* five hundred years old," Grenda said to Buck.

"Well, 537 to be exact," Buck told her.

"You sure don't look it," Grenda and Orell giggled.

A curtain fluttered at the rear edge of a balcony overlooking the great hall. Behind the curtain, whose flimsy material did little to block their view of the interview taking place below, Kane and the Princess Ardala exchanged words. Ardala had been observing the meeting between Buck, Von Norbert, and the three Draconian beauties, all alone. Now, unannounced, Kane stood beside her, his heavy presence obvious.

"Good afternoon, Princess," he greeted Ardala.

"You snuck up on me, Kane. Your standard mode of operation, of course."

"Not at all," Kane smiled his oiliest smile. "You were just too busy mooning over your pretty earthboy to notice my arrival."

"Be careful how you address your princess, Kane," Ardala snapped angrily. "Or I'll have your head!"

"Of course, Your Highness," Kane bowed, exposing the back of his muscular, bull-like neck for a moment, as if yielding to the request of a royal headsman. "I trust," Kane went on as he straightened, "that you and your imperial father have had a little talk. And you understand now that *I* am running things around here."

"Kane, I understand more than you can imagine!"

"Ah, Ardala, my princess. I do still want to be friends with you. You know I've always been very . . . fond . . . of my princess. I'm still willing to be your husband, in fact."

"The day the boiling sea of the Gregorian desert freezes over," Ardala returned.

"Well," Kane replied coolly, "till that day, then." He gave another sneering peek at the scene beneath their balcony, then strolled away, leaving Ardala to seethe.

While events moved at their accelerating pace on Villus Beta, the Inner City defense squadron continued to streak through warped space, Colonel Wilma Deering in the commander's position, Major Dylan in the executive officer's. There was a bleep from Wilma's commo telescreen and she flicked a toggle to activate her two-way audio-video circuit with Earth.

The wizened features of Dr. Huer appeared on her telescreen. "We've run your information to the computer council and they've confirmed your hunch," Dr. Huer said.

"I'm not surprised," Wilma told him.

"There's no truth to the claim that the Draconian race is dying out," Huer continued. "However, there is an area of the universe that the Draconians have been unable to conquer, probably because they have no immunity to the viruses of the sector. That part of space is called Gregoria. The council suspects that the Draconians are holding Buck in order to use his antibodies to secure immunities against viruses native to the Gregorian sector."

"Then it's all just part of their pattern for conquest," Wilma gritted. "Sounds like something Kane would do."

"Further," Huer said, an office light glinting from his old-fashioned spectacles, "the council and the Intelligence and Scanning Center have both calculated the results of the Draconians' capturing Gregoria. Wilma, child, it would give them an ideal position for an all-out attack against Earth!"

There was a long silence, broken at last when Wilma asked, simply, "What are my orders, Dr. Huer?"

"That is still being discussed here. Stand by, Wilma!" The hand of the figure in the vision screen reached for a control switch and Dr. Huer's face faded slowly from the screen.

In the great hall of Villus Beta, a casual observer would have thought that a casual party was taking place, rather than a serious genetic experiment— or an interstellar war!

Six persons lounged around a groaning board. Scraps and fragments of a sumptuous meal were in evidence, but even more than that the table and the floor around it were littered with empty and half-empty bottles, and the men and women still filled and emptied their goblets from time to time.

The three men present were Buck Rogers, Kane,

and Professor Von Norbert. Their three feminine companions, all of them decked in gorgeous, filmily provocative costumes, were none other than Grenda, Blorim, and Orell.

Kane, his wattled face and luxuriant costume spotted with spilled wine and dropped food, rose unsteadily to his feet. At one end of the table, her countenance darkened both by the shadows of the great hall and the misery of her state of mind, slumped a fourth woman: the Princess Ardala.

"To the professor," Kane toasted happily. "He has found the solution to our problem!"

"To the professor," Buck joined in the toast. He looked at Grenda, Blorim, Orell in turn. "I think I'm going to like his solution after all."

They drank—Kane, draining a huge goblet at one gulp, part of its contents running over his chin and down his neck to be soaked into the rich cloth of his costume.

"You are too kind," Professor Von Norbert said calmly. "It's Buck here we should toast. The solution lies in the blood that runs in his veins. To you, Buck." He lifted his own goblet.

They drank again, Kane refilling his goblet and emptying it again at a swallow. He turned a bleary eye toward Buck Rogers. "Not too much for you, Buck," Kane laughed. "We wouldn't want you to get too . . . drunk! Ah, ha-ha-ha-ha-ha!"

Orell smiled and leaned her cheek against Buck's shoulder. "We sure wouldn't want that," she cooed her agreement with Kane. Orell and the other two young Draconian women tittered in unison. From her corner of the table, the uncharacteristically subdued Ardala glared at the other three females.

"Buck," the professor asked, "which of the young ladies would you like to be sent to your quarters first?"

"What a choice," Buck replied. He ran his eyes up one lush body and down the next. "I never could choose between chocolate, strawberry, or vanilla ice cream, either!"

The three young women tittered again. The Princess Ardala winced.

"Why choose?" Blorim suggested, "we'll all go."

The three females tittered again, their coyness even less convincing now than it had been earlier. Ardala threw a goblet furiously across the hall. As it bounded and clattered on the hard polished floor, the princess jumped from her seat and stormed from the room to the adjacent indoor-outdoor garden. Buck Rogers followed her with his eyes, grinning all the while.

"I'd rather be a little more—personal," Buck commented in response to Blorim's suggestion. "You know, we're not machines, we're people. And we can't be mechanical about these things."

"Quite true," Professor Von Norbert put in.

"So, me Buck-o, what do you propose?" Kane asked with a belch.

Buck pondered briefly. "Why don't we go by alphabetical order? Blorim, then Grenda, then Orell."

"Great!" Blorim enthused.

Orell, pouting, said, "I never got to sit in the

front of the class at school, either. Why don't we use *reverse* alphabetical order for once!"

"I always wind up in the middle," Grenda complained. "And to think, I was almost named Alice."

"Girls," Professor Von Norbert took charge, "it is time for you to get ready. Off to your own quarters, now, and prepare!"

They scurried off, jabbering with excitement. As they left the great hall, each gazed back longingly at Buck. He waved to them good-naturedly.

"Ah, I'd kind of like to take a little stroll in the garden myself," Buck commented. "To prepare, you know."

"Certainly," Professor Von Norbert assented, "whatever you like, Buck."

In the garden Buck had taken hardly a dozen steps when he was halted by a voice speaking his name.

The Princess Ardala stepped from behind a giant flowing fern. "Buck," she asked him sadly, "how can you go through with this?"

"Through with what?" the earthman asked innocently.

"This inhuman . . . torture!" Ardala blurted.

"Gee," Buck mused aloud, "I never thought of it as torture, myself. Just something, well, expected of me. Sometimes I wish I had a different name than Buck."

"Well, you're torturing *me*," Ardala asserted. "Don't you know that?"

"How am I doing that, Princess?"

"Buck! Oh, Buck Rogers, I . . . I love you!" Ardala sobbed.

Buck stopped in mid-stride. "Oh," he commented.

"And I hoped that you had some feeling for me," Ardala added. "That night you spent with me aboard the *Draconia* . . . I thought . . ."

"Princess, it was very ungallant of me, I'll admit, but—you know, I doctored your wine that night. I gave you a Mickey. And I didn't sleep with you."

"I know. I know," Ardala admitted. "But I hoped that it could be different this time."

Buck turned to face her. "Princess, I have the highest respect for you. And you are—well, probably the most beautiful woman I've ever met."

"Then, take me!" Ardala demanded.

"Princess"—Buck flinched away from her—"I hardly know you!"

"But you don't know those women in there at all! Those women—I *should* say, those little girls. Silly, giggling five-year-olds."

Buck gazed at her, puzzled.

"You won't take me, but you're willing to . . . I don't understand you earthlings," Ardala resumed.

"Hey, I'm a prisoner here, you forget that?" Buck snapped. "I'm just doing what I'm told. This wasn't my scheme, Ardala!"

"But you act as though you liked the idea."

"Well, I'll let you in on a great big secret, Princess! It's a lot nicer to do this than to be locked up, starved, and tortured."

"You mean you don't really want to do what they've demanded?"

"Let me put it this way," Buck explained his

attitude. "I like this about as much as a sheep likes to give wool. It may not be his preference, but it's a lot better fate than getting turned into muttonchops!"

"If that's your real feeling, Buck, then I have a way out of this for you. Come away with me. Away from Villus Beta. I can get you out of here!"

Buck stood thinking deeply. Things were taking just the turn he'd hoped they would. And now he had to play his hand with skill! "Where could we go?" he asked innocently.

"Out of this sector altogether. Home—to my castle. We'd be safe from Kane there."

"But would we be safe from the Emperor Draco?"

"No," Ardala admitted bitterly. "No, we wouldn't. It's hopeless. Everyone else worships my father, but he's the bane of my existence. If only the Gregorians would kill him." She whirled. "Buck! *We* could kill him. You and I—we could do it together!"

"Princess, I'm a lover, not a killer. At least," he paused an instant, "the professor thinks so."

Ardala shook her head as if to clear it of cobwebs. "Then take me to Earth. I can get a ship for us. My father will never reach us there on Earth. We'll be safe in the Inner City!"

Before Buck could reply, the professor's voice sounded, calling to him as the scientist strode from the great hall. Unlike Kane, Von Norbert was a temperate drinker and had remained sober. "Buck! Are you there?" Von Norbert called.

Ardala gestured a message to Buck, hid herself

again in the foliage. Buck answered the professor. "Over here!"

"Very good," Von Norbert answered. "Well, young fellow, the time has come. Shall we proceed?" They strode off together. As they passed from Ardala's earshot, the professor said to Buck, "You haven't seen the Princess Ardala, have you?"

Buck said that he hadn't.

CHAPTER 15.

From his sparkling office in the Inner City of Earth, Dr. Huer placed another spacephone call to Wilma Deering. Colonel Deering was still seated in the cockpit of her star-warping rocket fighter. Their exchange was extremely brief—but vitally important to Earth!

"Wilma, child! We've determined the Draconian strategy, and Earth stands in dire peril. You *must* stop the Draconians from using Buck Rogers' antibodies. You must stop them at any cost! Even if it means the loss of—Buck Rogers himself!"

Wilma looked tragically at her telescreen where the living image of Dr. Huer gazed solemnly back at her. "Acknowledged," she said softly. With one graceful, trembling hand, Wilma Deering reached for the control knob beneath the visiscreen and wiped away the pink-faced image of Dr. Huer.

Blorim, quivering with eagerness and decked out in a costume that made her former brief attire seem puritanical by comparison, strode the corridors of Villus Beta, headed at last for the entrance to Buck Rogers' quarters. She was escorted by a guard, whose job it was to see that Buck did not

186

use the arrival of his guest as a means to make good his escape.

"What a lucky guy, that Rogers bum," the guard commented philosophically.

"This is a scientific experiment," Blorim countered.

"Well then, I wouldn't mind volunteering as a guinea pig!"

"Do you have any qualifications?" Blorim inquired.

"I'll compare my qualifications with anyone's," the guard told her. He halted before a door. "Anyhow," he continued, "here's the place."

"I was thinking of mental qualifications," Blorim told him as the guard hit the door controls and an opening swung aside before Blorim.

She stepped into the room and the door swung shut behind her.

Buck was garbed in a new outfit—rough, masculine, yet neatly cut of raw leathers. He had no shirt on, and the muscles rippled beneath the skin of his torso and arms. He held a bottle in one hand and two glasses in the other.

Suddenly shy, Blorim blurted, "Uh, hi, Buck."

"Hi," the earthman grinned back at her.

"Uh, I'm glad they didn't name me Zenor," Blorim said. "I don't think I could have waited!" She overcame her shyness as suddenly as she had been overcome by it, and ran to Buck. He was forced to hold his arms outstretched to keep the bottle and glasses from being knocked to the floor. Blorim threw her arms around his naked torso and began to plant little kisses all over his chest and face.

Bottle and glasses still clutched in his fingers, Buck closed his arms around Blorim's shapely body. "Uh," he stammered, "er, have a sip of this, ah, champagne or whatever it is," Buck offered.

"Champagne? What's that?" Blorim asked.

"Well, I don't know what they call it nowadays," Buck said, "but this stuff at least reminds me of champagne. Here, look!" He maneuvered her so she sat down—but she maneuvered him so it was the bed she sat on.

He handed her the two glasses, used his thumbs to work the cork gradually from the mouth of the champagne bottle. When he'd finally worked it loose, the cork leaped from the mouth of the bottle and flew across the room with a loud *pop!*

Blorim shrieked, then joined Buck as he laughed aloud. She held the glasses up and he leaned over, filled both of them with bright, bubbling fluid, then put the bottle down at his side.

"To us," Buck suggested.

Blorim accepted the toast. They drank—Blorim draining her glass at a single draught. Buck refilled her glass.

Buck said, "Your turn, now."

"My turn?" Blorim asked.

"To make a toast."

"Are you hungry?" Blorim asked. "Where's the bread?"

Buck laughed. "No, no, like this." He raised his glass and sipped at it. Blorim drank the contents of hers.

"He really believed me," Professor Von Norbert laughed, turning from the telescreen to Kane. "He discovered that we had his quarters bugged, and I promised to have them cleared, and the fool actually believed what I told him!"

Kane added his raucous laughter to Von Norbert's sneering chuckle. "Well, the fool—I just wish he'd get on with it!"

The two eavesdroppers turned their eyes back to the screen that showed the amorous situation slowly developing in Buck's quarters.

"These things do take time," the professor commented.

"Not for me," Kane asserted.

"That's what I hear," Von Norbert concurred.

On the screen—and of course in Buck's room as well—the muscular earthman was explaining to Blorim. "Now, you say, 'To . . .' something."

"Oh," Blorim acquiesced, "I see. Fine. To something."

"That's good enough for me," Buck commented. They raised their glasses. Buck took a tiny sip from his own as Blorim drained hers. He raised the bottle with his free hand, tipped it momentarily over his own glass as if pouring, then righted the bottle, leaned over Blorim's glass and poured it full.

"This is really good stuff," Blorim said as she drained her glass again. Each time she spoke her speech became more slurred. After quite a while, Blorim lay back on the bed. Buck caught her arm as she slid downward, took the empty glass from her limp hand and placed it on a table.

Then he leaned over Blorim, gingerly unwrapped her outer garment, a chiffon cape of Draconian design, and hid it under the bed.

"Blorim," he said to her, gently. "Blorim, can you hear me?"

With a tiny portion of her mind still functioning, Blorim managed an incoherent sound. "Huh?"

"Blorim," Buck almost shouted into her ear, "I want you to remember this. 'He was wonderful.' Remember. 'He was wonderful.'"

Blorim obediently repeated the words in her slurred voice.

Buck helped the semi-conscious woman to her feet. He managed to get her to the door. "Right, Blorim. Remember. 'He was wonderful.'"

"Wunn'ful," Blorim echoed drunkenly.

Buck pressed the latch, found the door unlocked. It swung open to reveal the same guard who had escorted Blorim to Buck's room. Buck virtually handed the helpless woman to the guard. "Could you help the lady get home?" he asked the guard. "She, uh, kind of—you know—a glass of wine, then too much excitement."

The guard reached for Blorim and she collapsed onto his shoulder. "He was wunn'ful," she slurred.

Half-carrying, half-dragging Blorim with him, the guard started down the hall. As he went he grumbled aloud. "Big deal."

Buck shut the door of his room from the inside. There was no point in making a break for freedom, now—there was nowhere to go on Villus Beta, and little chance of getting off the planetoid. Instead, Buck retrieved Blorim's wrap from under his bed. He tried it as a disguise—around his body, around his face. While he was experimenting there was a knock at the door.

Buck had barely time to get Blorim's wrap

hidden a second time when he found himself face to face with—Grenda!

"Hi, Buck," the second young woman said. "You know, I've never, uh, *been* with an earthman. If you know what I mean. Is it true what they say about earthmen?"

"I—uh—du-du-dunno," Buck stammered. "What do they say about me?"

She tried to say something and was held back by some small residue of propriety. Finally she advanced to Buck and raised her lips to his ear. She was wearing as exotic and as skimpy an outfit as Blorim had worn. Her coiffure, Buck noticed, was absolutely spectacular—and absolutely false. As she nestled up to him she knocked it slightly askew and had to reach up to fix it.

Finally she regained her composure and managed to whisper something in Buck's ear. He listened until his jaw dropped.

"No," he said loudly, "that's not why they call me Buck, Grenda!" He considered for a moment longer. "Well," he amended, "*maybe* it is. I never thought of it quite that way. But listen, what are you doing here? I thought you were on for tomorrow night."

"Tomorrow?" Grenda asked. "No. I was scheduled second, that's all—not second *night,* you silly. What about the rest of tonight? And when Blorim came back looking so happy, I thought I'd better come over here and take my turn."

"Oh," Buck said, deflated. "Well, uh—oh well, what the heck."

Grenda beamed up at him. "I'm ready." She

reached behind herself and began to undo her
costume. Buck backed away in confusion.

"Uh . . . wait," he said.

She looked at him with wide, innocent eyes.

"I mean . . . uh, would you like some champagne?" he asked. "That is, uh, Vinol. I'm sure I
have another bottle here somewhere. Or—we
could send out. I know a good deli down near the
Loop in Chicago, and. . ."

Grenda said, "No, thanks."

She reached for the light switch and plunged
the room into darkness. In the murk there was
nothing to be seen, but plenty to be heard. Grenda
all but dived into Buck's arms—arriving with a
thud that knocked the wind out of him. There
followed a series of words, moans, other sounds.

In Buck's voice, "Oooh."

In Grenda's, "Sorry."

A series of fumbling sounds, then in Buck's voice
again, so that one was not quite certain whether
he was expressing forgiveness or appreciation,
"That's okay."

There was a thump, as of two bodies onto a soft
surface, and in the voice of the body that landed
on bottom, a male body, a male voice, "Ow!"

And a female, "Sorry."

Buck said, once again, "That's okay."

There was a sound of rustling, other sounds,
some as of skin sliding on skin, some more moist.

A voice again, "Oooo."

Another, "Sorry."

A small light sprang on in the room, and Grenda
said to Buck, "Why did you do that?"

"Because I want to see you," he answered. "You're beautiful, you know, Grenda."

"So are you," she cuddled against him.

As Grenda pressed her cheek to Buck's naked chest, she could feel his hand on her back . . . caressing her neck . . . sliding up under her wig. She raised her head from his chest to give him a quizzical look.

"Don't stop what you were doing," Buck suggested.

Grenda shrugged. She put her face back down onto his chest and kissed the muscular flesh there.

Buck carefully slipped Grenda's wig from her head and gently spread her real hair across his shoulder. She smiled up at him. He slid the wig under the bed. With one hand he continued to caress her; with the other he carefully opened her purse, slipped her lipstick and makeup from it and slid them under the bed, then closed the purse again.

He bent his head so that his lips were pressed against Grenda's ear. "Are you sure you wouldn't like some wine?" he whispered in her ear.

She shook her head negatively.

"Uh, maybe a game of cards? Some bright conversation?"

She sat up angrily, glared into his face. "What's the matter with you? Can't you keep your mind on what you're doing?"

"Oh," Buck stammered. "Well, uh, you see—uh, Grenda, well, I really do like you a lot. And you're a beautiful person and all, but—well. . ." He stopped speaking.

She stood over him, hands on her hips. "But, well, what? Don't earthmen do it the same way everybody else does?"

"Oh, er, sure," Buck managed. "It's just that—oh, well, maybe some other time, Grenda. I'll try and make it up to you."

"The hell you will!" she snapped. "I've got a couple of things to say to that creep Von Norbert for the buildup he gave you. Now, where are my clothes? Okay! And where did my wig go?"

"What wig?" Buck asked.

"I had one on when I came in here."

"Are you sure?"

"Of course I'm sure, damn it!"

"Well, I'll keep a good eye out for it, Grenda. If a wig turns up anywhere, I'll let you know about it right away."

"Thanks a lot," she said. She strode to the door and jerked it open angrily. "Listen," she said, turning back just before she left the room. "There's one thing I'd like to ask you, Captain Rogers."

"What's that?" Buck inquired.

"Why *do* they call you Buck?"

In the telescreen room, Kane and Professor Von Norbert had both passed out and lay sleeping soundly before the screen. The room was warm and stuffy, the upholstery soft and comfortable, and as for the titillating display of eroticism they had expected to witness—well, who can blame them for falling asleep.

Still, had they remained alert they would have seen the inside of Buck Rogers' room after Grenda's departure. Buck checked the door, began searching the room. Was he looking for Grenda's missing wig? Hardly! He knew where that was.

He crept around the baseboard of the room, checked all the ventilator inlets and outlets, pulled away a grille and found—the second monitor camera! He pulled it from its place, snapped the lead that carried power to it and images and sounds away.

In the telescreen room, the panel that carried the video image went blank and the loudspeaker that carried its audio counterpart hissed into silence. Von Norbert and Kane snored away.

Buck Rogers stood before a mirror in his room, carefully—if somewhat clumsily—applying to his face the makeup that he had extracted from Grenda's purse. He did the best he could, then slipped the purloined wig over his own close-cropped hair. Finally he slipped Blorim's wrap around himself. He examined himself in the reflecting panel.

Well—he wasn't exactly a ravishing beauty, but —he might pass muster in a dark alley at midnight.

He strode to the door, reached for its catch when—it opened in front of him and Orell stood there staring. She screamed. He grabbed her with one muscular arm and pulled her into the room, shoving the door closed behind her with his other hand.

Orell gaped up into his face. "I'm—I'm—it's my turn!" she gasped. "Who—who are you?"

Buck thought as fast as he could. "Don't you know me?" he asked after a moment of silence.

"No," Orell shook her head. "You're not from Villus Beta, I'd recognize you if you were."

"That's right," Buck said in a weak imitation of a female voice.

"Then you must be one of Princess Ardala's ladies-in-waiting."

"Yes, that's right," Buck said, trying still to sound like a woman. "The princess is claiming her royal prerogative. A princess gets her way, you know. You'll have to wait, dearie."

"But where's Buck?" Orell demanded.

"He went to the princess' chambers," Buck explained, improvising as fast as he could. "He'll be back here afterward. He'll send for you when he's good and ready."

Orell started to leave, crestfallen. Then she turned back and planted her feet firmly on Buck's floor. "Good and ready, hey?" she said. "Well, I think I'll just wait for him right here!"

Buck flounced past her to the door. "If that's the way you want it, dearie, that's fine with me. Ta-ta!" He opened the door, stepped into the hallway and shut it again behind him. He started down the corridor, past the bored and sleepy guard.

"Hey, I thought I just saw you come out o' there," the guard exclaimed, shaking his head blearily.

"Ha-ha!" Buck said in his falsetto voice, "I went back for some more. That Rogers is really something! *Ciao!*" His heart pounding with every step, waiting for the guard to figure things out and command him to halt—or zap him with a laser—Buck continued down the corridor.

By the time he rounded a corner and knew that he was out of sight of the guard, he was covered with sweat—but he was safe, at least for the moment! He made his way carefully through the by-ways and corridors of Villus Beta, avoiding contact with anyone he could avoid, making his exchanges with those he could not avoid as brief and impersonal as possible.

His closest call came when he was stopped by a guard who put his hand on Buck's arm and swung him around under a ceiling light. Buck was ready to slug the guard and make a run for it when he realized that he wasn't being interrogated as an interloper—the guard was making a pass at him!

Buck barely managed to keep a straight face as he flirted briefly with the guard, suggested a rendezvous in the nearby garden, and sped away from the encounter as fast as his flimsily clad legs could carry him!

But one aspect of the strange encounter stayed with Buck as he put distance between himself and the guard.

"Are you a real woman?" the guard had asked.

Buck had thought he was caught, but he brazened it out. "Why—aren't you a real man?" he responded.

"You know what I mean," the guard said. "Are you a regular kind of woman—or one of those five-year specials?"

"Five-year specials?" Buck echoed, puzzled.

"You know," the guard said. "Those ones with the special accelerated growth hormones. The ones they're making for the Gregorian war." He looked at Buck in annoyance. "Don't act like it's such a secret, honey. Everybody on Villus Beta knows. If you're one of those specials, it's okay with me. If they're big enough, they're old enough, that's my motto!" He leered and petted Buck on the arm.

"Oh, ah, everybody knows about it, hey?" Buck managed to get out. "Er, of course they do. Well, if you must know, why, yes, I'm one of the specials. I didn't think you could tell, big boy."

"I couldn't, believe me, sweetie. I just kind of guessed. You look terrific for a five-year-old. I seen some of the early models that went all wrong. It was a sad sight to see, too!"

Gradually Buck was coming to an understanding of the complete ruthlessness, the disregard for humanity, of the Draconian leadership. Kane's callousness was of course obvious. But Professor Von Norbert, beneath his distinguished appearance and scientific demeanor, was at heart no better than his partner!

The guard was still smiling at Buck, thinking him a woman—or pseudo woman. "I get off duty at six," the guard said. "Wanna meet me then?"

"Oh, I can't wait that long," Buck cooed. "I'll meet you in the garden in about two minutes. How about that?"

"But I'm on duty! I can't leave my post—they'd court-martial me!"

"Tough luck," Buck twitted the guard. He turned away, tossed a final seductive look over one shoulder and flounced away.

CHAPTER 16.

By royal prerogative, the Princess Ardala had been assigned a sumptuous suite of rooms, not in the bowels of the wedge-shaped city of Villus Beta, but on the surface of the planetoid. She left her curtains open a crack, so the splendid celestial sights of the Villus system were visible in the depth of night. The double sun of Villus was of course shining its light on the other side of the planetoid, but from Ardala's bed she could, if she awoke in the night, watch the splendid dance of the asteroids as they drifted eternally in their complex, interlocking orbits.

A number of the smaller mini-planets had been captured by each of the larger ones, and swung around their primaries like miniature moons, sending rays of pale light dancing over the surface of every object they could reach.

Ardala, dressed in a voluptuous nightgown that would have served to tempt the most jaded of appetites, tossed restlessly in her huge, satin-sheeted bed. She was only partially wakeful, but some sound, some evidence of motion in the room penetrated her sleep-fogged senses.

She sat upright suddenly. There was someone

in her bedchamber! She reached under an over-stuffed pillow and drew out a tiny laser-pistol. She was wide awake now! "Stop where you are!" she snapped into the partial darkness. "I have my laser pointed right at—"

But a powerful hand crashed into her graceful wrist. She managed to retain her grasp on the pistol and squeeze off a blast, but the beam went far wide of the mark, burning an ugly scar into the fancywork of the wall.

"Ardala!" a manly voice exclaimed. "It's me, look!"

The powerful hand kept its grip on her wrist. With his other hand the stranger reached through the murk and flicked on a room light. Ardala stared at the person who had invaded her room— apparently a woman, clad in a set of filmy, sexy garments.

"Who?" Ardala asked.

The stranger smiled.

The princess studied the smiling face. "Buck?" she stammered. "Buck? You're *very* pretty!"

Buck lifted one hand self-consciously to the wig he had stolen. "Thanks, Ardala, but I don't have time for compliments. Are you ready to go to Earth?"

"Yes," Ardala replied. "Oh, yes. Look what I got for you. I was going to hunt you up and give it to you in the morning."

She reached under her pillow again and brought out a gleaming, plexiglass rectangle.

Buck looked at the object, recognized it and smiled happily. "Theopolis!" he exclaimed. He reached for the computer and Ardala handed him its carrying strap.

"Theo, you old devil," Buck said happily as he hung the strap around his neck. To Ardala, Buck said, "This is really great! This is going to simplify our escape a lot. I wanted to get Theo back and I didn't know where he was. And I really didn't want to face the computer council back on Earth without him."

"We can sneak out of here and get a ship right now," Ardala suggested. She climbed out of her bed and started toward the window.

"Not yet!" Buck stopped her. "We have to get to the main computer room first, and tap the big system for information on my family."

"No," Ardala demurred. "There isn't time. We have to get off this planetoid and out of this whole sector of space, fast! Kane, or even my father, might be after us at any moment!"

"We'll have to risk that," Buck insisted, "I came here for something and I'm not leaving without it. This whole affair is the result of my search, and I won't quit now!"

Reluctantly, Ardala yielded. Instead of climbing from her window, Buck insisted on their using the door to the main corridor. Ardala was astonished not to find a guard there. "What did you do," she asked Buck, "kill him?"

"No," the earthman said, swirling his feminine chiffon. "I seduced him. He thinks he's keeping a rendezvous with me right now."

They made their way through darkened corridors and deserted halls. As they went, Buck carried on a whispered conversation with Ardala.

"You people haven't been exactly honest with me about this antibody matter, have you?" Buck demanded.

Ardala played innocent for starters. "What do you mean?"

"I mean you don't need them to save your race from extinction. You need them to conquer Gregoria!"

"Yes, that's true," Ardala conceded. "But it wasn't my idea, Buck, you can believe me. It was all Kane's idea, Kane's and Von Norbert's. I'm blameless!"

"Sure you are. And Mayor Daley was a Republican."

"What?"

"Nothing," Buck grumbled.

They continued onward. Most of the corridors were vacant at this hour of Villus Beta's night. But not all! When Ardala and Buck, both of them in seductive female attire, passed Draconian guardsmen, the guards acted solicitous. They were respectful of the princess' position as daughter of the emperor and heiress-apparent to the throne of Draconia. They were also men who appreciated a beautiful woman when they saw one—or thought they saw two!

Buck halted in the anteroom of the main computer center, grasped Ardala by the wrist again and pressed her against the wall. In the princess, instincts fought—she resented being manhandled, forced against her will to stop, go, do anything that she did not choose to do . . . but at the same time she enjoyed the contact and the implied interaction with Buck Rogers.

"What is it?" Ardala demanded in a low voice.

"There's something else I have to get straight before we round this last corner—just in case we get zapped inside there." He inclined his head toward the main computer room.

"What is it?" Ardala asked her question a second time.

"I want to know about this business of raising people in five years. My would-be boyfriend asked if I was a regular woman or one of the five-year specials. What's that all about?"

"There's a new set of hormones that Professor Von Norbert invented. They speed up the growth and maturity processes."

"Then—if I father children for Draconia, children with those vital antibodies in their bloodstreams—they'll be all grown up in five years? In five years they'll be troopers going into combat against the Gregorians?"

"That's right!"

"And what about those girls they sent to me—Grenda, Blorim, Orell. They're only five years old?"

"Yes and no," Ardala temporized. "They're five the same way you're five hundred. They have all of the development and maturity of grown women —but they got it in five years."

Buck rubbed his chin with his free hand, pondering. "Okay, you've got a point there, Ardala. Okay. Let's get on with this."

They turned the corner and strode into the computer room itself.

Two guards, uniforms sparkling and neat, weapons at the ready, stood at the door. At the approach

of outsiders they were immediately on the alert,
but as soon as they recognized the Princess Ardala
they dropped their hostility and snapped to a crisp
salute. Buck still in wig, makeup, and women's
clothing, hung back so he could be seen but would
not draw attention away from Ardala.

"My Princess!" the senior of the two guards
blurted. "May we be of service to Your Highness?"

"Yes," Ardala commanded coolly, "you may let
us pass."

"I'm sorry, Your Highness. We are allowed to
admit no one without authorization."

Ardala nodded. "Very proper of you. Very well,
I hereby grant you authorization to let us pass."
She looked over her shoulder at Buck, intoned
imperiously, "Come along, I will need your assis-
tance."

Ardala and Buck strode past the two guards,
who stood aside with their weapons returned to
their holsters. As they were almost into the computer room the second guard gathered all of his
courage and ordered them to halt again. "I beg
pardon, Your Highness, but I'm sure you wouldn't
want us to disobey our orders. Mr. Kane and Professor Von Norbert ordered us to let no one pass
who wasn't on the list they gave us. I don't believe
that your name is on it, Your Highness."

"Mr. Kane and the professor work for me,"
Ardala said sharply.

"Yes, of course, Your Highness."

"Very well. I am adding my name to the list,
effective now."

"Very well, Your Highness, if you put it that
way. Your name will be on the list. But, er, I'm

afraid that your lady-in-waiting will have to re-main outside."

"My lady-in-waiting is my closest friend and assistant. She goes where I go. But if it will help your conscience to rest easier, put her name on the list, too. It's—Bussy Exer."

"Yes, Your Highness." Again the guard stood aside, and this time Ardala and Buck entered the computer room. Behind them, the automatic atmo-sphere-seal doors hissed softly shut.

"Wow!" Buck exclaimed. "You brought that off beautifully, Ardala! Thanks!" He embraced her. From Buck's side, the embrace was one of friend-ship and gratitude. From Ardala's, it was—some-thing else!

Buck slipped from Ardala's arms and slid into the operator's chair at the main control console of the computer bank. He keyed in a series of com-mands through the typewriterlike device that held center position at the desk-type console. The computer's indicator panels sprang to life, reels of tape whirred, readout screens glowed eerily.

"Hurry," Ardala urged. "That guard is going to decide to cover his tracks sooner or later by checking our story out with Kane. Once that happens we're in the soup!"

"I'm going as fast as I can. Is there any faster way to work with this piece of iron?"

Ardala leaned past Buck, flipped several control knobs on the console. She pressed the input-mode button for *oral*, held her hand to the pattern-reader, said, "On oral. Princess Ardala. Go ahead." She turned to Buck. "Put your hand where I held mine."

He complied.

"Captain Buck Rogers," the computer's electronic voice intoned, "pilot, Inner City, Earth. Though you sure don't look it today! Proceed."

Buck gave a startled exclamation at the machine's unexpected comment. Then he turned serious. "I want access to your data-banks. I need all available genealogical information on my family."

"Please be specific in your inquiry," the electronic voice responded.

"I want everything you have."

"Buck," Ardala interrupted the dialogue, "we don't have time to argue all night with a computer. And even if we did, we surely won't have time for a whole long readout."

Buck thought. "Wait a minute, then." He addressed the computer input again. "Are you compatible with a compuvisor? Can you feed data directly into his storage bank so I can get it back out later?" Buck held Theopolis against the computer console's pattern-reader. The small computer's indicator panel lights all came on.

There was a moment of tense silence, then the big computer said, "Yes. Compuvisor model one-four-eight-zero is compatible with my output format. Data-transfer procedure initiated—now!"

The main computer's indicator panels flashed, then lights flicked off one by one as the information was fed through a direct computer-to-computer linkage into Dr. Theopolis. In less than a minute the big computer's indicator panel was dark. The synthesized voice announced that the transfer was complete.

"Right," Dr. Theopolis confirmed, "I've got it

all. Say, that's a nice computer there. I really enjoyed chatting with him."

"So you *can* still talk," Buck scolded Theopolis.

"Yes, but not to strange women," Theopolis replied.

"Thanks," said Buck.

"Let's get out of here," Ardala urged. "If you've got what you want, you can play quiz with that toy later on."

"Toy!" Theopolis protested.

"A term of royal affection," Ardala soothed him.

"Well, that's better, then."

"Okay," said Buck, "let's go. Say good-bye to your big playmate, Theopolis, and we'll head for the spaceport." He gave Theo a moment to commune with the big machine, then flicked the giant computer's master switch off and climbed from the operator's chair.

Buck and Ardala—with Theopolis still hung around Buck's neck—set out a second time through the hallways and chambers of Villus Beta. This time they were headed for the spaceport by the most direct possible route. Time after time they passed Draconian guardsmen, and each time the princess brazened out any challenge by citing her royal credentials and threatening any recalcitrant guard with reassignment to the stoker gang.

They didn't know where Wilma Deering was. Buck and Ardala both had witnessed her blastoff in the captured starfighter, but they had to assume that she would return all the way to Earth and then gather a rescue force from among her own command. They didn't know about the Ellis

Plan; they didn't know that the Inner City defense
squadron was already speeding at top star-warp
acceleration toward Villus Beta.

Nor did they know the whereabouts of Kane
and Professor Von Norbert. The partners in—if
not crime, then something hardly distinguishable
from it—had long since dozed in front of the telescreen trained on Buck's private room. They didn't
know that Buck had found their second monitor
camera, or that the last of Buck's five-year-old
"girlfriends," the voluptuous Orell, still sat impatiently on Buck's bed, awaiting his return from
his rendezvous with the Princess Ardala.

But the professor and the courtier Kane might
awaken at any moment, and once they did, a
certain sequence of events must follow as inevitably as the chain reaction that follows the attain-
ment of critical mass in an imploding nuclear
device.

They would see the blank telescreen. They
would suspect that Buck had discovered and disabled the second monitor camera. They would
hurry to his room to confirm that he was present.

Instead of Buck and a voluptuous mating-
partner, they would find the impatient Orell sitting alone on Buck's bed. They would question
her and Orell would tell them that Buck had gone
to a meeting with the Princess Ardala—or at least
that one of the princess' maids had told them as
much.

So the chain of events would develop, link by
inevitable link.

Kane and Von Norbert would next head for
Ardala's private suite of chambers. They would

find her missing, sound a local alarm, learn from the guards that she and a companion had consulted the central computer facility and left.

And then they would sound a general alarm—if they hadn't done so earlier in their sequence of inevitable events.

Buck and Ardala stepped out of the mouth of the elevator tube at the entrance to the Villus Beta spaceport.

They were met by a team of Draconian guardsmen.

"Princess!" one of the Draconians exclaimed. "We didn't expect to see Your Highness here."

"Well, here I am!" Ardala snapped. "I've no time to chat. Let my maid and myself pass at once."

"But I have my orders, ma'am," the guard insisted. "No one may pass without the express authorization of Chancellor Kane."

Ardala tried to use the line which had got herself and Buck past the guards at the computer center. "Kane is *my* chancellor," she announced imperiously. "He can give commands only by my authority, and I have the authority to override those commands as well. I order you to let us pass."

At the computer room this tactic had worked. At the spaceport, it failed. "I'm sorry, ma'am. I can't unless I hear it from Mr. Kane himself, ma'am."

Ardala seethed. "I will give you one more opportunity, soldier. You and your partner here step aside and let us pass, or you might as well turn in your uniforms and draw stoker-gang outfits right now."

"I'm sorry, Your Highness. I can't do it."

Ardala drew back one arm, balled her fist and let fly at the guard.

He staggered back, more startled by the fact that the princess had actually taken a punch at him than he was by the stinging force of the blow itself. The second guard stood equally thunderstruck, uncertain whether to go to the aid of his companion or to give his attention to Princess Ardala.

As the two guards stood frozen in a moment of indecision, Buck Rogers launched himself through the air at the second of them. The guard had drawn his laser-pistol, but the force of Buck's muscular body pounding against his chest sent the weapon clattering to the tarmac.

Ardala rushed to the skittering pistol and scrambled to grab it while the second guard grappled futilely with Buck and the first, recovered now from the princess' blow to the jaw, drew his own laser-weapon and pointed it at Ardala.

"You dare aim a weapon at your princess?" Ardala screamed at him imperiously.

The guard, confused, turned instead to point his weapon at Buck. He would have fired off a bolt, but Buck and the second guard were locked in a struggle, rolling and thrashing about on the tarmac.

While the first guard stood pointing his laser at Buck and his foe, frantically striving to find an opening for a shot at the earthman, Princess Ardala calmly pointed the laser-pistol that she held at the first guard. She coolly squeezed the trigger. There was a flash of light as the guardsman took the laser bolt at point-blank range.

With a look of astonishment in his eyes, he sank slowly to the ground, his knees crumpling beneath him, his laser-pistol clattering from his hand.

Ardala advanced the few steps that separated them, picked up the guard's weapon, and walked back to the place where Buck and the second guard were wrestling. For the moment Buck was on top, but the guard with a mighty heave threw the earthman off him and started to rise to his feet.

In that instant Ardala fired a second laser blast, sending the guard crashing back onto his skull and shoulders. He lay unmoving, a few yards from his equally stationary companion.

"Well now," Ardala said to Buck, "that takes care of that. Here"—and she tossed him the second of the two laser-pistols. "I doubt that we'll have any more trouble," Ardala continued, "but if we do, we'll not have to bandy words any longer!"

CHAPTER 17.

Chancellor Kane and Professor Von Norbert strode through the corridor leading to Buck Rogers' private room. The inevitable had happened. They had awakened and discovered the blank telescreen connecting them—or, more accurately, *not* connecting them—with Buck's quarters.

A guard, standing at attention outside the door to Buck's room, snapped a proper salute to the chancellor and the professor at their approach.

"Everything all right, guard?" Kane demanded.

"Fine, sir, yes, sir."

Kane strode past the trembling guard and shoved the door open. He looked inside and spotted Orell sitting disconsolately on the edge of Buck's unmade bed.

"Where's Rogers?" Kane demanded.

"I don't know," Orell wailed. "He was supposed to be visiting the princess but it's been so long, I wonder if he's ever going to come back here at all!"

"The princess?" Kane echoed.

"Yes," Orell's lower lip quivered, "you know, the *princess*, that beautiful, sexy Princess Ardala!"

Kane whirled furiously to confront the guard. "I

thought you told me everything was all right here," he roared furiously.

"Yes, sir," the guard quavered, "it is. Er, isn't it? Sir?"

"I'll 'sir' you, you damned jackass! Rogers is gone!"

"But he can't be, sir. I mean—he didn't leave. I'd have seen him, sir."

"You idiot! Come with me!" Guard in tow and Von Norbert trailing breathlessly behind, the burly Kane set off through the corridors toward Princess Ardala's suite.

At the spaceport, Ardala and Buck raced across the field to the nearest ship. "Can you pilot that?" Ardala panted, pointing to a large, sleek rocket ship, a D-III.

"I can pilot anything on this field!" Buck snapped. "I don't mean to sound conceited, but I've done a lot of test-piloting—flying a new ship is nothing to me. If I can't handle it, it hasn't come off the line yet!"

They clambered through the hatch, made their way to the bridge of the powerful craft. Ardala pointed to the control panel of the ship. It was studded with hundreds of dials and levers, screens, knobs, and switches. "How do you feel now?" she asked Buck. "Are you still so sure of yourself?"

Buck's eyes gleamed happily. They contained an expression, as he let them rove over the instrument panel of the spaceship, that Ardala had longed to see in them when Buck looked at her.

"Am I ever," Buck said. "Can *you* run this thing?" he asked the princess, impishly.

"I hire people to do things like that," she replied.

"Well then," Buck grinned, "you just hired me." He sat down in the pilot's seat, began to study the controls. "Of course," he muttered with just a trifle less confidence in his voice, "it'll take me a little while to figure out what some of these gadgets and doohickies are *for*, but I'll get the hang of it pretty soon."

He ran his hand through his hair. "I think so, anyhow," he added.

Suddenly lights sprang into full, glaring life all around the ship. Their glare penetrated the thick, polarizing viewports of the cruiser, blinding Buck and Ardala. They both rubbed their eyes, slowly regaining their sight.

Emergency sirens wailed. Squads of mounted soldiers roared across the tarmac in groundcars and armored personnel carriers. Other squads followed on foot, dog-trotting to reach the ship as quickly as possible.

Kane, in an emergency command post set up at the edge of the field, roared commands to Draconian officers who jumped to obey, sending enlisted personnel scurrying off in all directions.

Inside the spaceship, Ardala said, "They've found us out, Buck. There's no more time to study. If you think you can fly this ship, get us out of here right now. Otherwise they've got us stopped."

Buck swung toward her, the boxlike Theopolis still nestled against his chest. "What then?" Buck asked. "If they get us now, what happens?"

"I don't know what happens to *you*," Ardala said. "But as for me, I tell Draco and Kane that you kidnapped me at laser-point and forced me onto this ship at the risk of my life!"

"Okay," Buck acknowledged, "that's just what I wanted to know. Hang on, Ardala, 'cause—as we used to say back when I was a kid—here goes nothing!"

He set the control levers by the time-honored method of Kentucky windage, leaned his full weight into the main firing stud, and prayed.

Slowly, majestically, the heavy ship lifted away from the tarmac. Her exhaust flames spread like a sheet of fire, turning squads of Draconian troops and vehicles into smoking, charred black cinder.

Then, with a sudden rush of acceleration, the ship seemed to leap away from the inverted wedge of Villus Beta. She balanced there in the planetoid's sky, a shining bird with a glowing, wavering, fiery tail. Then there was another burst of acceleration, and the ship disappeared into the night of deep space.

The emergency command post that Kane had set up at the edge of the Villus Beta spaceport had become, in effect, a War Room. The chancellor, Professor Von Norbert, the commander of the Villus Beta detachment of the Draconian Guards, all huddled. Kane was clearly in charge— Von Norbert served to answer questions of a scientific nature, the guard commander took orders from Kane and passed them on to the weapons squads under his control.

"Use the beams," Kane gritted. "Quickly, before that ship goes into star-warp, before it's out of our range."

"Are you sure he has the princess aboard with him?" Von Norbert asked uncertainly.

"Yes." Kane didn't equivocate.

"But we didn't actually see her climb into the ship. Maybe. . ."

"She's with him, you old fool. Stop dithering!" Kane commanded.

"But—but you can't shoot their ship down if she's aboard," the guard commander protested.

"Why not?"

"The princess! She's . . . she'll be . . ."

Kane roared with laughter. He turned to the guard commander. "Do as I told you, man, or I'll throw you out and get someone who will! Turn loose all batteries against that ship before it gets away from us."

"Wait a minute, Kane." It was the professor pleading now. "We can't destroy that ship. We *need* Buck Rogers. The whole Betan project . . . the whole Gregorian campaign . . ."

"I don't care," Kane shouted him down. "That man Rogers has defied me, he's thwarted me, he's taken the princess from me for the last time. And for the last time, commander—fire those batteries and do it now!!!"

"We made it, Buck!" Ardala leaned over the pilot seat of the stolen cruiser, put her arms around Buck Rogers' neck and squeezed affectionately. His hands were occupied on the controls of the ship as Ardala planted a big, juicy kiss on his cheek.

"I thought you were ready to turn me in, Ardala," Buck said in annoyance.

"But that was only if they caught us," Ardala explained. "If we got caught anyhow, why should I get in trouble? You're a very strange man, Captain Rogers.

"And we didn't get caught!" She stood up again and danced gaily around the cabin. "We made it! We're free! We're—"

Her ecstatic exclamations were interrupted by the flash and crackle of a full battery of laser bolts as they zapped past the cruiser and disappeared into the void.

"Whoa!" Buck Rogers exclaimed. "Looks as if we aren't so clean away from Villus Beta after all!" He'd tossed aside his stolen wig, wiped off the feminine makeup that he'd worn. In place of the filmy Draconian harem-clothes he'd used to escape, he now wore a proper space-pilot's attire looted from the ship's stores in the past few minutes.

"They must be crazy!" Ardala exclaimed. "Or—maybe they don't know that I'm aboard!"

Another volley of bolts zipped past the ship. This time the ship was grazed by the edge of the volley. It shuddered, its hull glowing briefly with the raw, raging energy of the bolts.

Buck was knocked sideways by the charge that reached his hands through the controls of the ship.

Ardala ran to the pilots' seats, jumped into the co-pilot's chair and swiftly righted the spaceship before it could go into a helpless—and possibly fatal—tumble through space.

With a gasp Buck recovered himself. "Maybe

they're firing at us because they *do* know you're
aboard, Ardala!"

"Never mind that. Quick, which control gets us
into warp?"

Buck reached, set a dial, flicked a toggle and
leaned on an activator stud.

Nothing happened!

"What's the matter?" Ardala demanded. "Hurry
—before they really get hold of us with a bolt!"

Buck broke out into a sweat. He reached, reset all the ship's warp controls to neutral, took a
test reading, reset them again to plunge the ship
into that strange region between normal space
and null-existence, leaned hard on the activator,
grunting with effort as if he could nudge the ship
into warp-space by sheer expenditure of will
power.

Still nothing happened.

"Sorry, Princess," Buck told Ardala, "I'm afraid
that near-miss was much too near and not enough
of a miss. They got our warp-generator with the
power-surge. We can still fly this thing like an
old-fashioned chemical rocket ship, but warp is
out for us."

"No!" Ardala screeched. "No! Oh, that Kane!
I'll have him and his cronies killed forty times over
for this!"

"How?" Buck asked. "From your sanctuary on
Earth? With me?"

There was the crackle and flash of another volley
of laser bolts. This time they passed even closer
to the ship. The glow of the power-surge lighted
up the whole cabin, turning Buck and Ardala
nearly into glowing neon statues of themselves.

When the surge passed, Buck and Ardala crumpled
to the floor of the ship. The lights dimmed within
the cabin as the ship's power systems began to fail.

On Villus Beta, Kane and his cronies—as Ardala
would have called them—followed the wild ef-
fects of their one-sided war through electronic
telescopes. When the second blast grazed the
speeding ship Professor Von Norbert exclaimed
in anguish.

"You'll have to answer to Draco himself for
this, Kane! Don't you see—you're as crazy as
Draco's crazy daughter! You're both so caught up
in your dreams of vengeance that you can't see
the facts.

"Please, Kane—call off this attack. You're going
to be responsible for killing the emperor's daughter
—and for losing the whole Gregorian campaign!
Think of having to face Draco after all that!"

Kane held his head in his hands. His hatred and
rage were no less than ever, but the hysterical
violence of the moment had gradually faded away,
and he was able to exercise his wily powers of
deduction once again.

"All right, Professor. Guard Commander—call
off the laser attack. Prepare to launch a fleet of
Draconian fighter rockets. I'll lead the flight myself, and we'll bring back those malefactors alive
—to face the wrath of Draco the emperor, and of
Chancellor Kane!"

Princess Ardala moaned and moved her arm
slowly. She lifted her head and looked around the
bridge of the cruiser. The ship's power system was

off but the cabin was lighted faintly by the clear radiation of distant stars. She could see Buck Rogers lying a few feet away from her.

She reached out to Buck and shook him by the shoulder, at first gently, then, when he failed to respond, more vigorously. "Buck," Ardala demanded, "Buck, are you alive?"

A low moan escaped the lips of the earthman. He stirred and looked at Ardala blearily. He shook his head and sat up.

"Buck," Ardala throbbed, "we're going to die. This is it, I know it. But at least we're together for the end!"

Buck set his jaw resolutely. "Don't be so sure, Ardala. This may not be the end." He dragged himself forward, crawled under the ship's main instrument panel, opened a door and reached inside. He worked for a few minutes, then closed up the panel again.

One by one the ship's lights were flickering back to life. In a few minutes the wildly tumbling craft had regained its steadiness. "You see?" he asked. "Good design, this ship. Proper replication of all systems. Redundancy features. We're off and running again. But—why haven't they fired another bolt? They had us reeling. . . ."

"I don't know," Ardala whimpered.

"Maybe they've called off their attack," Buck mused. "Maybe they decided to let us go."

"Fat chance!" Ardala complained. "Besides, even if they're through with us—I'm not through with them!"

CHAPTER 18.

A useful maxim in time of war is: *Never underestimate your enemy.*

Another is: *Never confuse moral judgments with estimates of military capabilities.*

What all of this means is that good guys sometimes beat bad guys, but they don't do so just *because* they're good guys. They win out because they're stronger, or smarter, or braver; bigger, tougher, more committed, more ruthless, quicker, more numerous . . . sometimes, just because they're luckier.

But moral superiority seldom has anything to do with victory—if only because there's seldom been a war in history where *both* sides didn't think they were on the side of the angels and their opponents on the side of the wicked.

Kane sprinted across the tarmac of the Villus Beta spaceport and vaulted through the hatch of the command ship of the Draconian squadron waiting on standby. He reached back and dogged the hatch shut, strapped himself into the pilot's command seat and checked out the launch-readiness of the craft. As he'd expected—Kane was a

221

tough and demanding military commander—the ship was in prime condition, ready to launch at the pressing of a firing stud.

Kane flicked on his commo set, cleared with launch control by the simple device of ordering the controllers to scrub all other priorities, and commanded his squadron to follow him into space.

The entire inverted wedge of the city of Villus Beta, and in fact the entire miniature world, trembled in response to the titanic forces unleashed by an entire squadron of space-fighters launching in rapid-fire succession.

Almost instantaneously the Draconian ships streaked for their positions in pursuit formation, Kane's ship in the lead spot, the rest of the squadron spiraling out behind him into a formation that could have made a giant ice-cream cone, headed narrow-tip-first away from the tiny world.

The visual sighting of Rogers' and Ardala's ship as it sped away from Villus Beta had set a target for the Draconian squadron. Once spaceborne the squadron locked onto the remote quarry via a full range of automatic devices: electron telescopes, tightbeam radar sweeps, mass detectors. The D-III was far larger than any of the Draconian fighters —they were designed, after all, as high-speed mobile weapons-platforms, with minimum space or weight allowances set aside for creature comforts, while Ardala's ship was an armored space cruiser replete with living quarters and large-capacity life-support systems designed to sustain passengers and servants as well as flight crews.

Aboard the cruiser, Buck Rogers was manipulating the control levers that managed the ship's

main exterior visiscreen. He had made the takeoff
from Villus Beta via a combination of direct
optical sighting and the proverbial seat-of-the-
pants that born pilots could always rely on in a
pinch and others could never hope to develop.

But now, Buck was struggling to get the visiscreen working so he could work out long-range
navigational plots. The screen was not of a model
that Buck had used before, its controls were not
familiar to him. "How do you get this thing tuned
up?" he asked Ardala.

From her position beside Buck, in the co-pilot's
command chair, Ardala simply shrugged her
shapely royal shoulders. Buck continued to wait
for a more expressive answer. Finally Ardala said,
"I imagine you just ask the communications officer
of the ship's crew."

Buck snorted angrily. "I'm afraid we forgot to
bring the commo officer along with us."

"Well, you're the one who bragged about being
able to fly anything in space," Ardala sneered.
"Try living up to your boasts."

Buck fumed but returned to the control levers.
He finally hit the right combination, got an image
on the screen, continued to work at the job until
he was able to control it as he wished. The picture
that he finally settled on was a long view of deep
space, with remote stars and even more remote
galaxies picked out against the black background
of nothingness.

"There," he said with satisfaction. "That's what
lies ahead of us. We can plot a detailed orbit later.
Right now, at least we're not going to smash into

any chunk of space debris or otherwise get ourselves in trouble."

"Well, goody-good for us," Ardala said sweetly.

Buck flicked a control lever and the image on
the screen flipped to another picture of deep space
—this time, the region from which they had
emerged. The tiny shape of Villus Beta was still
visible in the center of the screen, shrinking visibly
as the royal cruiser sped away from it.

Buck leaned forward, peered closer into the
screen, turned the field-of-vision control to zoom
in on the center of the previous image. "*Uh*-oh,"
he breathed, "that's either the most unusual event
in the history of astronomy—a bunch of tiny little
stars have left their orbits and are chasing us—or
else Kane has launched a pursuit squadron of his
own and they've followed us from Villus Beta!"

Ardala leaned toward the ship's control console,
bringing her dark eyes closer to the screen and at
the same time accidentally—or perhaps not accidentally—pressing her soft curves against Buck
Rogers' muscular arm. She looked at the image
of the Draconian pursuit ships and made a sound
of contempt. "*Pah*! There's no way they can catch
us. This ship can outrun them easily."

"I'm afraid not," Buck said slowly. "Not without
warp capacity, and those laser surges we took
before seem to have wiped out our warp drive.
We were lucky that the main drive of the ship was
duped, but warp hardware is too bulky and heavy
to carry a dupe set of, even on a cruiser!"

"But then—what can we do?"

Buck flicked the visiscreen control and restored
the view of oncoming space he had used before

looking back toward Villus Beta. "They have warp and we don't, so there's no way we can outrun them. But maybe we can outsmart them."

From the Draconian pursuit squadron's lead ship, Kane peered deeply into his own visiscreen. The D-III cruiser loomed large in the center of the screen, and under the constant, thunderous acceleration of Kane's ship's pulsating power plant, the cruiser was slowly but steadily growing larger and larger.

Suddenly the cruiser veered from its straight-line course. The ships were far beyond Villus Beta of course, and almost to the limits of the Villus system altogether, but small objects still circled in orbits of their own. One such—it might have been a small planet, an unusually large and dense comet, or even a planetoid drifting at the aphelion of an unusually eccentric orbit—appeared at the farther edge of Kane's visiscreen.

Before Kane's amazed eyes, the cruiser swerved toward the remote planetoid. It flashed toward the object, appeared for a moment as if it were going to crash head-on into the rocky object, and then—disappeared!

Kane rubbed his eyes. "What happened?" he demanded over the commo-net to the pilot of the pursuit rocket nearest his own.

"I—don't know, Chancellor," the pilot babbled. "Did they crash into that planetoid? But there was no flash, no flareup as their fuel supply went. They couldn't have just . . ."

"Maybe they disappeared into a black hole," another pilot ventured his opinion.

"What do you think?" Kane demanded.

"Don't know, Chancellor," the pilots in Kane's squadron chorused across the commo-net.

The chancellor was furious. "What kind of spacemen do you call yourselves? What kind of Draconians? You've got to do something! Quickly!"

"Yes, sir," a particularly courageous rocket pilot answered. "Has the chancellor a suggestion as to *what*?"

Aboard the cruiser, Ardala and Buck watched the Draconian pursuit fleet flash by, headed away from the star Villus and toward the void of space. "How did you do that?" Ardala asked Buck admiringly.

"I guess they don't give Draconian pilots much training in astronomy—just what they need for astrogation, which is part of the story but not all of it by a long shot. Every object, including that weird chunk of rock"—he pointed out the viewport at the nearby planetoid—"every object that orbits a star casts a cone of shadow in the direction *away* from the star. That's what causes eclipses. When a planet, say, passes through its own moon's shadow. Or vice versa."

"Argh! Stop! I don't want astronomy lessons," Ardala shrieked at Buck. "I want to know what you did to save us from Kane just now!"

"Well, that's what I was just telling you," Buck smiled calmly. "I just ducked our ship into the shadow of that planetoid. To Kane and his men, it looked as if our ship just disappeared. We don't even show up on their mass detectors—we blend right in with the planetoid and they get a single reading for *us* and for *it*!"

He laughed happily as the Draconian ships shrank to tiny, dwindling points in the remote distance.

"All right," Ardala snarled, "however you did it, Captain Rogers, they're gone. Now, we will return to Villus Beta. Kane and the rest will give up and return to Beta eventually, but we'll be there waiting with a hot reception when they do!"

Buck stared at the princess. "But, Ardala," he exclaimed. "I thought we were headed for Earth! It'll be a long trip without warp drive, but we could still do it. What happened to your pledges of eternal love for me?"

"Never mind! Just turn back! I, the princess, command it!"

"No, ma'am!"

"No? Did you say *no* to me? A princess?"

"Yes, ma'am. That is, yes, ma'am, I said no, ma'am," Buck explained.

Without another word Ardala drew the laserpistol from the waist band of her gown. She pointed it at Buck. He pulled his hands from the spaceship's controls and reached to grapple with Ardala for the weapon.

Buck was the stronger and more agile of the two, but Ardala started with the advantage of both the weapon and the first move. They tussled back and forth, swaying dangerously over the delicate controls of the royal space cruiser.

Suddenly there was a flash of light, a puff of black, acrid vapor.

Buck Rogers collapsed to the floor and lay unmoving. The computer brain, Theopolis, that had hung from his neck tumbled away from the man, skidded a few feet across the floor and lay flashing incoherently.

Ardala seated herself in the pilot's command chair and reached for the ship's controls. She hesitated, her hands above the controls, then tentatively tried readjusting them. She had told the truth about knowing little of space flying. She was indeed a princess, and had servants and retainers ready to jump and do her bidding at any task, any time and anywhere in the Draconian realm.

What need had she of such practical education as learning to pilot a rocket?

She tried a guess, shoved a lever, turned a knob, leaned onto an activator stud.

The ship lurched wildly and began to spin around. The impetus of its new power setting sent it tumbling out of the shadow of the planetoid where Buck had carefully placed it in a parking orbit. Distant as it was from the sun Villus, still the ship's brightly polished metallic skin caught the distant star light and scintillated with it, like a new tiny star in its own right.

One of the pilots in Kane's pursuit squadron was scanning the Villus system behind his ship. As the cruiser came tumbling from the shadow of the planetoid, the pilot exclaimed, "I see it, I see it! Chancellor, behind us, quadrant Q-14, at seven o'clock!"

Kane flashed his visiscreen control to pick up the newly visible space cruiser. "There she is," he muttered. "Now, I wonder what tricks that sneaky pilot Rogers and Ardala are planning to pull on us now!"

From the control bridge of the D-III cruiser, Ardala could see Kane's pursuit squadron returning, zeroing in on her own craft. She slapped frantically at control switches and knobs, struggling desperately to stabilize the cruiser and attempt an escape.

Instead the lights flickered, the ship's trembling and tumbling increased. Ardala abandoned her futile efforts to work the flight controls and instead threw herself onto Buck's inert body where it lay on the flight deck. "Wake up!" she demanded. "Buck! I didn't mean to shoot you! You've got to help me, Buck!"

The spaceman groaned. At least he was alive!

But Ardala was unable to get him to his feet, unable to get him to resume control of the cruiser.

She looked up, desperately aware that the Draconian space ships were closing in. She couldn't see into the cabins of Kane's and the other ships, couldn't see the pilots, working under Kane's command, transfer the bulk of their power from their own propulsion systems into tractor beams that they locked, one after another, onto the big cruiser.

Slowly the power beams from the Draconian fleet took effect on the bigger ship. To the Princess Ardala, accustomed to having her every directive put into effect by eager underlings, the new motion of her cruiser was a delayed response to her own efforts to bring the ship under control. The cruiser's trembling and tumbling smoothed out;

she began slowly to move through space on a new, orderly path, far in advance of the Draconian fighters.

Her eyes wide and bright at the sight she misinterpreted, Ardala shrieked with triumphal laughter. "I did it," she almost screamed. "I did it myself! What do I need with stupid men?"

She turned away from the control console and stood over Buck Rogers' inert body. She drew back her royal foot and delivered a vicious, scornful kick to the unmoving spaceman.

Then the cruiser swung gracefully through space, starting to fall into formation with the Draconian pursuit squadron. Gradually it dawned upon Ardala that her efforts had not saved her or the ship at all—that she was being taken in tow by some invisible, intangible, irresistible force.

Ardala could not see the face of Kane, nor could she hear his words. But her vivid imagination conjured up a graphic—and basically accurate— image of his oily features distorted into a horrifying, triumphal grin. Her mind could summon up the sound of his raucous laughter and his scornful expressions of triumph as the royal cruiser came into formation with the Draconian fighters, from all outward appearances the flagship of a mighty fleet but in actuality a helpless pawn being dragged back to Villus Beta to face a fate best left unspeculated upon.

With a frantic cry, Ardala hurled herself upon the body of Buck Rogers once again. From love to scorn to hopeless dependence was the wild course of Ardala's feelings for the earth-born spaceman. Now she needed him once again, and now she returned to her frantic pleadings, urgent demands that he rise, take control of the cruiser, help Ardala to escape the clutches of Kane.

But Buck Rogers did not move.

Instead, the big cruiser swung majestically into her position at the apex of the cone of Draconian pursuit ships. With equal majesty the whole formation swung around, pointed like an arrow in the direction from which all of the ships had originally come, and began moving with increasing speed back toward the spaceport at Villus Beta.

CHAPTER 19.

On the telescreens of the starfighters of the Inner City defense squadron led by Colonel Wilma Deering, a formation of points of light swung into view. They were shaped—the formation, that is, for each individual light was merely a glowing dot—like a giant geometric cone.

Each of the points of light that made up the cone was of an identical brightness—indicating that the objects they represented were of the same size and mass—and an identical color—indicating that they were of the same composition.

The Inner City starfighters' computers analyzed the points and their readout screens identified them. The pilots of the starfighters, under the new policy instigated since the arrival of Buck Rogers and his induction into the squadron, independently analyzed and identified the screen images. They checked their own conclusions against those of their ships' computers, and agreed on the identity of the lights: Draconian high-speed spacefighters.

There was one exception to the uniformity of objects: the lead ship of the Draconian squadron, the point of the spiral, was far brighter and differently colored from the others. Again the pilots racked their brains while their computers analyzed the image and shuffled through the electronic equivalents of file cards trying to identify the single exceptional point of light.

"I think that's a Draconian D-III freighter," one of the pilots ventured over the radio net. "Might actually *be* a freighter—though I don't see why one would rate that kind of fighter escort —or it could be a basic D-III frame modified into a space cruiser."

"I think that's it," Colonel Deering answered the pilot. "Check your computer readouts, all pilots."

Every starfighter screen indicated Draconian D-III configuration.

"It might be a command ship or a royal cruiser. Same as that ship we spotted over the Inner City shield a while ago," Wilma said. "Okay," she resumed, "let's head into action!"

In Kane's Draconian ship, a voice boomed over the radio. "Inner City fighter squadron dead ahead, Chancellor. What are your orders—shall we attempt evasive maneuvers?"

"Evasive maneuvers!" the massive Kane roared. "Great sizzling sunspots, no! Turn around! Fight the sniveling weak earthers! Blow those ships out of the heavens!"

"But—they probably won't attack us," a Draconian voice said.

"They'll certainly not attack us if we blow 'em out of the sky first," Kane replied.

"But, sir! If we switch over power to combat maneuvers and laser torpedo action, we might lose control of the princess' cruiser. It takes a lot of power to tow a D-III."

"Worry about that later. Now's fighting time, you pig!" Kane snarled into his radio.

"Yes, sir. Here we go. Switching power to laser torps. Ready, on my mark—commence fire!"

On the telescreens aboard the Inner City starfighters, the spiral-shaped formation of Draconian craft suddenly sprouted a whole new set of tinier, moving dots of brightness. The dots separated from their parent ships, headed away from the spiral formation and toward the starfighters.

"Draconian laser torpedoes!" an Earth pilot cried into the radio commo-net of the starfighters.

"All right," Wilma Deering gave her instructions, "all starfighter pilots, prepare to dodge hostile fire. Commence evasive maneuvers—utilize defensive pattern A."

The formation of Inner City fighters swerved in mid-space, with the uniformity and precision of a corps of precision swimmers.

The Draconian laser torpedoes passed among the Inner City ships, for the most part passing harmlessly at high speed and soaring away into space to join the eternally floating jetsam of the interstellar void. A few of the torpedoes, their mass-activated proximity fuses responding to the passage of starfighters, exploded.

Some did so harmlessly.

Others rocked starfighters with the sheer, savage power of their charges.

Wilma Deering was briefly shaken as her ship escaped a laser torpedo with a near miss. Wilma flicked on her radio, spoke into the tiny microphone. "Good work, starfighters. Another volley of laser torps on their way. Switch to pattern W for evasive maneuvers."

Again the starfighters swung gracefully through a complex pattern of evasive action. Again most of the Draconian torpedoes sped past the starfighters, some of them exploding as their proximity fuses picked up the nearness of the little rocket ships.

This time, however, one of the laser torpedoes scored a direct, head-on hit against a starfighter. The laser-charge of the torpedo and the fuel and weapons supply of the starfighter vaporized in a huge blossoming explosion. In the vacuum of space there was of course no sound, although the starfighter pilots in the rest of the Inner City craft picked up a monstrous burst of electrical interference through their radios at the moment of detonation.

Circuit-breakers went out on a dozen visiscreens and had to be reset manually after the incredible flash had died away to a slowly fading and contracting glow.

A few of the pilots had taken direct radiation exposure through the viewports of their ships, and would carry skin burns back to med-bay from the engagement, submitting to anti-radiation sickness therapy lest they become delayed casualties of the present battle.

One of the Inner City pilots took a readout from his craft's situation monitor. "That was ship number 14 that got it," he read into his microphone.

"Acknowledged," Wilma Deering said in a low

voice. "That was Mark. He's gone. All right, it's obvious that no parley is possible. Let's prepare to launch weapons in counteraction.

"Ready—arm torpedoes."

Aboard every starfighter, pilots were clicking over brilliant red switches from "stand-by" to "armed."

"Three—two—one—" Colonel Deering counted down.

In every starfighter, thumbs poised over launch buttons.

"Fire!"

A swarm of deadly hornets sped from the starfighters toward the Draconian interceptor ships. Deadly hornets, yes—but each hornet was a laser torpedo, each of them housed not in the carapace of an insect but in the ply-formed housing of a weapons container; each was propelled not by a pair of whirring gossamer wings but by a miniature fusion-reactor in its tail.

And each carried as its sting, not a bloated sack of chemical venom, but a sealed generator of pure, ravening radiation, ready to escape at the first opportunity—to send an enemy ship tumbling through space, reduced to white-hot fragments and glowing radioactive vapor.

The Draconians threw their ships into evasive maneuvers of their own. Most of the Draconians escaped with little or no damage, but two of the fighter craft sustained fatal hits, exploded and spun away, bearing their pilots to certain death and perpetual preservation in the absolute frigidity and utter vacuum of outer space.

The massive D-III cruiser that led the Draconian formation was rocked by a near miss. The tractor beams of the Draconian pursuit craft had been cut by now: those craft needed all the power and all the control they could muster to hold their own in combat engagement with their Inner City adversaries.

As the cruiser resumed its tumbling through space, the Princess Ardala resumed her frantic ministrations, pleadings, and demands addressed to the semi-conscious Captain Buck Rogers.

Hysterical now, Ardala dealt the spaceman a stinging slap on the face.

Buck snapped around, a look of fury on his face at the pain and the affront he had suffered. But in an instant he took in the situation and made a frantic dive across the cabin, into the pilot's command chair again. He began hurriedly slapping at control switches, shutting down one system after another throughout the ship.

"What are you doing? What are you doing?" Ardala cried frantically.

"Killing our power!" Buck yelled back at her.

More and more laser torpedoes were passing near the royal cruiser. A series of them blasted in quick succession, all but engulfing the rocking, quivering ship in a seething sea of flame and radioactivity.

"Buck!" Ardala yelled. "I don't understand! Why are you cutting all the power in our ship?"

"We're caught between two forces," Buck shouted. "There's no way to escape, so I'm going to play dead. If they think we're done for they may stop firing at us!"

The last of the D-III's power system faded

away into darkness. In the deep of space an eerie
sub-twilight illumination filled the cabin of the
ship, punctuated by frequent, blinding glares of
light as torpedoes exploded near or on contact
with fighter craft.

"Is this the same ship that brought me to Villus
Beta?" Buck shouted at Ardala.

She thought for a moment. "Yes!" she replied.

Buck scrabbled in a concealed compartment behind a circuit panel beneath the console. He found
what he was looking for after a few seconds of
searching: it was a miniature line-beam transmitter that Ellis 14 had provided him on Earth.

Buck examined the transmitter. "This is what I
wanted—we may get out of this yet. But the
power source is all shot. How can I—?"

Without waiting for the help that he knew
Ardala would never provide, Buck scrambled under the console and began to strip away the in-
sulation from a major power cable. He pried open
the casing of the line-beam and jury-rigged a connection between the little transmitter and the
D-III's main power system.

"This is crazy," Buck said. "Listen—we tapped
in onto a peculiar inductance flux and we're getting radio signals on the line-beam."

In a faint, distorted tone overlaid with constant
loud cracklings, Buck and Ardala heard the conversation taking place between Colonel Wilma
Deering and the senior pilots of the Inner City
defense squadron.

"Colonel," a man's voice said, "let's all zero in
on that Draconian D-III lead ship. Blast the

damned space barge right out of the known universe!"

"But I'm not getting any power reading from it. The ship seems to be dead," Wilma Deering replied.

"I think they're playing possum," another pilot interposed.

"Could be," Wilma acknowledged.

"Then let's blast it."

"All right. Al, read me the coordinates."

There followed a series of space-location statistics.

"All ships ready to fire."

"Hold fire while I check them for radiation again. I want to double-check my line-beam tracker," Wilma's voice said.

Aboard the Draconian cruiser, Ardala shrieked, "Buck, can't you get that thing working? They're going to blow us up!"

Buck struggled frantically. Why didn't the transmitter function?

Buck pried the front panel off the little transmitter. Somehow a tiny beetle had crawled into the device and got itself electrocuted. How could that be? Probably all the way back at the Great Salt Lake? At least, that was when the insect must have got into the machine. It might have stayed alive indefinitely, and just accidentally shorted two leads and crisped itself at any time!

"If I try and clear that while there's power coming in from the outside leads. . ." Buck grunted. "But there's not time to take this off-line and put it back. I'll have to—

"—risk—

"—it!"

He managed to clear the charred bits of electro-cuted insect from the transmitter. There was a brief surge of power, Buck pulled his hand back as if it had been stung by a hundred spiders at once, but the transmitter clicked on, its signal flooding the nearby volume of space with a loud, clear beacon of its whereabouts.

"Hold on!" Wilma Deering shouted into her space ship's radio.

"Hold fire," a dozen voices echoed back to her from the rest of the starfighter pilots.

"I've picked up a line-beam transmission," Wilma said excitedly. "The only line-beam any-where near this sector of space is the one that Buck Rogers took with him from the Inner City. He must be on that D-III hulk!"

"I don't think so," another pilot snapped. "If the transmitter is there I think it's some sort of trap."

"You may be right," Wilma admitted. "But we can't risk killing Buck. All starfighters, switch to magnetic tractor beams and take the D-III in tow!"

For a second time the damaged space cruiser bearing Buck Rogers and the Princess Ardala was taken in tow by a squadron of smaller fighter rockets. But this time it was the Inner City de-fense squadron that took the ship in tow rather than the Draconian flight stationed at Villus Beta spaceport.

The Inner City ships locked onto the D-III, formed a globular nest around it, and began moving slowly back in the direction in which they had come.

The Draconian fleet, outweaponed and out-fought by the Inner City squadron, had been par-tially destroyed in the exchange of laser torpedoes. The Draconian pilots had turned back toward their home base. Briefly Kane had tried to rally his followers, then he too decided that discretion was the better part of valor and turned back toward Villus Beta, leaving the cruiser—with Rogers and the princess—safely in tow by the Inner City squadron.

Aboard the D-III cruiser, Buck and Ardala sat side by side in the pilot's and co-pilot's command chairs. The ship was still dark, only the little line-beam transmitter drawing power from the ship's reserve supply and sending out the beam that the earth ships focused on.

Ardala turned slowly to Buck, looking into his face in the semi-darkness of outer space. "What will they do with us, Buck? Once we reach Earth, I mean."

"I don't know. You may be tried for war crimes, Ardala. But more likely you'll just be interned and given back to your father."

"Never!" the princess gasped. "One is as bad as the other!" She pulled out a laser-pistol, pointed it at the bodice of her satin gown. Before she could pull the trigger Buck had vaulted from his command seat and wrestled the gun from Ardala.

Suddenly the connecting door from the D-III's airlock to the command bridge swung open. Wilma Deering, pistol in hand, strode into the room.

"Buck!" Wilma Deering cried. "You captured her!"

"And you won the space battle, Wilma! I didn't even know you'd docked your fighter to this ship."

"Oh, Buck," Wilma sobbed, her voice rich with emotion and relief, "we almost blasted you out of the sky!"

"But you didn't, and that's all that matters."

Buck and Wilma, each still holding a laser-pistol, moved as if to embrace.

"Welcome," Princess Ardala interrupted the reunion. "Welcome, my loyal friends from planet Earth!"

Buck turned back to Ardala. "Princess, you get on the radio and tell your friends from Villus Beta that you're going with us. If they had any plans to renew their attack, they'd better just cool off!"

"Do you have transmitter power?" Wilma asked.

Buck shook his head. "Can we tap your ship's supply?"

Wilma agreed.

"You tell Kane and Von Norbert that you're in control here, and if they interfere you'll kill Buck Rogers," Buck said, grinning.

"What?" Wilma Deering exclaimed.

"They want me alive," Buck said. "As long as I'm okay, even if I escape there's always a chance they can get at me again. But if I should get zapped—they can forget their big experiment."

Wilma burst out laughing.

Even Ardala smiled to herself as she picked up the microphone to transmit to Kane the message Buck had given her.

With a final click from the space radio, Kane

ended his raging tirade of frustration and defeat. Ardala hung up the microphone and turned back toward Buck and Wilma.

Wilma Deering looked at the princess, then turned toward Buck. "Now," Wilma Deering asked, "what do we do with her?"

Buck looked toward Ardala. "You want to come back to Earth with us or not?"

Ardala stood facing Buck and Wilma. The two Earth people stood with their arms around each other, holding affectionately to one another as they awaited her answer.

"I never want to go to Earth," Ardala said. "Never—until I visit as the mistress of a conquered province!"

"All right," Buck answered. "We can just leave you here."

"That will be fine. I would prefer it, my gallant captain."

"Do you think the Draconians will come back for her?" Wilma asked Buck. "Ardala can live for quite some time in this D-III, even though it's little more than a hulk. We can get some power up for her before we go, and there's plenty of air and food supplies left in this ship. But there's no way she can *go* anywhere. If the Draconians don't rescue her, she's stranded."

Buck considered. "Well, they are a little peeved by Ardala's, let's say, mercurial temperament. Not to mention her ability to switch her loyalties every time it's convenient. But then, that's a common Draconian trait, isn't it?

"Besides," he went on, "Kane is still looking for entrée into the royal household, and every now and then they do remember that Ardala here is the emperor's daughter. They'll come for her. Don't worry about making a female Robinson Crusoe out of Ardala, Wilma."

He turned to the dark-haired princess. "Well, good-bye, Ardala. Perhaps we'll meet again."

Ardala heard the statement in angry, smoldering silence. When Buck finished speaking she took the few steps that brought her face to face with him. Her face assumed a strange expression.

As Wilma Deering stood by, watching in astonishment, Princess Ardala leaned forward, turned her face upward, and kissed Buck tenderly on the mouth.

When Ardala stepped back again, Buck and Wilma started for the cabin door. At the last moment Buck sped back into the cabin, retrieved the dormant plexiglass box containing Dr. Theopolis, and carried it carefully to the airlock.

In the airlock Buck looked closely at the computer brain. "I think he'll need some work when we get back to Earth," Buck said to Wilma. "But I'm sure they can get him fixed up and scheming away as good as new."

The lights on Theopolis' indicator panel flickered faintly, and a sick voice moaned from his voder-synthesizer compartment. "A couple of aspirins and a good night's rest and I'll be as smart as I ever was," Theopolis groaned.

CHAPTER 20.

As the monorail sped sleekly from Earth's chief spaceport, the Inner City landing field, Buck Rogers and Wilma Deering sat comfortably in the streamlined car's form-fitting chairs. "I'm glad you sent Theo right off to the repair depot," Wilma said. "I'd really miss the old computer if we didn't have him fixed."

"They said it would only take a little work to get him blinking again," Buck said cheerily. "I expect he'll be delivered to my quarters by the time we finish our appointment with Huer."

The monorail glided smoothly to a stop. Buck and Wilma left the car and made their way into Dr. Huer's outer office. They were greeted by Lisa 5, the secretarial robot.

"Buck, Wilma . . . I mean, Colonel Deering and Captain Rogers. It's so good to see you both back safe and sound."

Wilma returned the greeting casually, with a "Hi, Lisa 5."

Buck was more demonstrative. "It's good to see you too, you little mechanical minx! How are things coming along with your friend Ellis 14?"

Can a robot blush? One would hardly think so,

unless it—or she—had special circuits built in to perform just that function. But it seemed to Buck and Wilma that Lisa 5 managed just that. "Ellis is the hero of the robot population," Lisa 5 said proudly.

"I'm not surprised," Buck supplemented Lisa's comment. "Wilma's—Colonel Deering's exec told us on the way back that Ellis invented the method they used to figure out where the Draconians were holding us. If it hadn't been for Ellis, we might still be stuck on Villus Beta!"

"Isn't Ellis wonderful," Lisa 5 cooed.

"Is your boss in?" Wilma Deering asked. "I'd love to stay and chat, but I think Dr. Huer is expecting us."

Before the secretarial robot could make any reply, the inner door opened and Dr. Huer strode through it. He was wearing his customary informal lab outfit, and his old-fashioned lens-and-earpiece spectacles. "So," Huer exclaimed happily, "the prodigal two return! How are you both?"

He grabbed Buck and Wilma and embraced both of them.

"It's so good to be back," Wilma said.

"Yeah," Buck agreed, "to plant our feet firmly under good old mother dome once again!"

"Well," Huer checked his electrochronometer, "personally speaking, I'm famished. Can I buy you two youngsters a bit of lunch? Maybe share a carafe of Vinol?"

"I think I'd just like to rest up a little," Buck excused himself. "But some day real soon now, Doc! Our official debriefings are one thing, but you're entitled to a little more personal version of the past few weeks."

"Okay," Huer acceded. "Any time you feel up to it, Buck."

"Say, what about me?" Wilma faked a pout. "I'd *love* to be your date, Dr. Huer."

"Wonderful!"

"Okay," Buck said, "you two have fun. I'll see you later."

He left, grabbed a monorail to the electronics repair center, and retrieved Dr. Theopolis. The robot brain was functioning better than ever—his indicator panel flashed on and off more brightly than Buck had seen it in all his days in the Inner City.

"What did they do to you, Theopolis? Looks to me like they did more than just replace a burned-out fuse."

"You can bet on that," Theopolis supplied. "Say, where are we headed?" Buck had hung the computer from his neck and climbed aboard the monorail once more.

"Just back to my place," Buck answered. "You can never tell when you're going to have visitors around here, and I don't want to turn up missing if somebody comes by I want to see."

Theopolis accepted that and rode quietly until Buck strode through the door of his personal dwelling unit and put Theo gently on the pillow of his bed. Buck pulled up a chair and sat beside the bed.

"Listen," Buck said to Theopolis. He was definitely blushing as he spoke. "Uh—I've never said anything like this to a machine before, Doc, but, ah . . . I'm sorry, Doc. I was really way out of line when I gave you away. When I traded you, you know, to the gypsy Pandro. I thought it was justified in a higher cause, you know?

"But you can't just treat people that way. I mean—I know you're a machine, Doc, but you're people, too. I'm sorry."

Theopolis blinked his lights for a long time. Finally he said, "I accept your apology."

"Thank you," Buck said. "Now, you remember all the stuff that you got from the big computer on Villus Beta?"

"Do I ever," Theopolis enthused. "What a wonderful machine! If ever I get back to that little planet, I'm going to look up the comp center and see what I can see."

"Uh, yes," Buck replied. "But I mean, Doc, ah— the genealogical data that was transferred from the big computer's memory bank into yours. . . ."

"Yes?"

"Well—what this whole thing was all about," Buck stammered. "My family—you know? Please, Doc?"

"Captain Rogers, you know what I'm starting to realize?" the computer said. "You only want me for my brain!"

"Damn right," Buck agreed.

"Very well," Theopolis said. He cleared his throat—or did the electronic equivalent of clearing his throat—and started to recite the data he had acquired on Villus Beta. "Rogers, William, a.k.a. Buck, born 1951, Chicago, Illinois. Lost while on space mission, local solar system, 1987. Known relatives: James Rogers, father; Edna Rogers, mother; Frank Rogers, brother; Marilyn Rogers, sister . . ."

The computer droned on.

And on.

And on.

Several hours later Buck had removed Theopolis from the pillow and placed him on the chair. As Buck put it, "You don't have the same sensors built into your ventral planar casement surface that I have in my *gluteus maximus*. You take the chair for a while and *I'll* take the bed." Buck then settled comfortably on his back, arms folded happily behind his head as he nestled into the pillow.

"Ah, that's fine," Buck exhaled. "All right, Doc. Resume the recitation if you please."

The computer started naming relatives and giving biographical statistics once more. Eventually he reached the year 2487 A.D. ". . . Which brings us to the present geometric computation of your descendants, Buck," the electronic voice droned, "in the proportion, after five centuries at an average breeding age of 22.76321, of some 86,000 to one—"

There was a sudden, loud knocking on the door.

Buck turned his head and called lazily, "Come in."

The door opened and Wilma Deering stepped into the room.

"Hello, Buck," she greeted. "You said you'd see me later, and here it is, later. You *did* mean me, didn't you? Or did you have Dr. Huer in mind?"

Buck rose from the bed and embraced Wilma. "Which do you think?"

They exchanged a brief kiss. Wilma reached

behind her with one hand and shoved the door shut.

"Nobody ordered this," Wilma said. Buck looked puzzled for a moment—then, comprehending, he grinned.

"You know what this all means?" Wilma asked Buck. "No perfumed fountains, no phony waterfalls or piped-in music? Not"—she looked around the room—"any bowls of fresh cold fruit, even?"

"It means anything we do, we do because *we* want to," Buck said.

"Right! Give that man a prize!"

"I already have one," Buck countered. They broke off their embrace but took the few steps across the room hand-in-hand. They seated themselves on the edge of Buck's bed and kissed again. The kiss turned into a rather extended clinch. At one point Wilma opened her eyes and happened to glance at the chair next to the bed.

There was Dr. Theopolis, indicator panel blinking on and off in a regular pattern as he observed all that took place before his optical sensing devices.

Wilma reached to the chair, picked up the computer brain and turned it so the indicator panel was on the opposite side from herself and Buck. As were the optical sensors!

As Wilma turned dreamily back to Buck he shoved himself upright on one elbow. "Wait a minute," he exclaimed. "I'm not really so sure of this after all. You know, Theopolis learned a lot about my relatives from that Draconian computer. And he's been telling me all about it today."

"Yes?" Wilma asked, annoyed. "So?"

"So," Buck explained, "in five hundred years, the computer says that any given person's descendants intermix with *other* people's descendants, the number of offspring and collateral relations increasing to the point that the 'I' of five hundred years ago would have no fewer than 86,000 descendants."

"Uh, huh," Wilma yawned.

"And," Buck went on, "the 'you' of *today* would have had no fewer than 86,000 ancestors five hundred years ago! You see?"

Wilma shook her head. "No."

"Well, what I'm saying," Buck explained, "is this. That, uh, while it hasn't been determined with certainty, Wilma, well, you see, in terms of mathematically determined statistical probability, that, ah—"

"Are you saying that I'm your granddaughter?" Wilma exclaimed. She jumped off the bed and faced Buck with fiery eyes.

"Yeah," Buck conceded miserably. "Well, not my granddaughter, of course. Something more like my great-great-great, ah, you know. . . But, yes. That's just about it."

Wilma thought about that for a moment.

"I don't give a damn!" she said succinctly, and jumped back onto the bed.

Buck rubbed his chin thoughtfully.

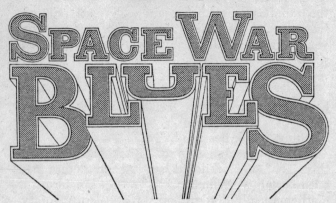

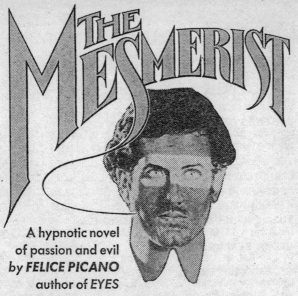

THE MESMERIST

A hypnotic novel
of passion and evil
by FELICE PICANO
author of *EYES*

In the Spring of 1899, a stranger came to Center City.
He was young and handsome—but his dazzling smile and
diamond-hard stare concealed a dark and deadly power!
Too soon, Center City was in his debt; too late, it was in his
power. Terror gripped Center City like pain, and only the
mesmerist knew how it all would end—and why . . .

"Compelling!"—*Chicago Tribune*

"The reader is pulled into the horror of minds in jeopardy.
A gripping, well-written tale!"—Mary Higgins Clark,
author of *Where Are The Children?*

A Dell Book $2.25

Dell Bestsellers

☐ **THE ENDS OF POWER** by H.R. Haldeman
with Joseph DiMona $2.75 (12239-2)

☐ **MY MOTHER/MY SELF** by Nancy Friday $2.50 (15663-7)

☐ **THE IMMIGRANTS** by Howard Fast $2.75 (14175-3)

☐ **SLAPSTICK** by Kurt Vonnegut $2.25 (18009-0)

☐ **BEGGARMAN, THIEF** by Irwin Shaw $2.75 (10701-6)

☐ **ASYA** by Allison Baker $2.25 (10696-6)

☐ **THE BENEDICT ARNOLD CONNECTION**
by Joseph DiMona $2.25 (10935-3)

☐ **BED OF STRANGERS**
by Lee Raintree & Anthony Wilson $2.25 (10892-6)

☐ **STORMY SURRENDER**
by Janette Radcliffe $2.25 (16941-0)

☐ **THE ODDS** by Eddie Constantine $2.25 (16602-0)

☐ **PUNISH THE SINNERS** by John Saul $2.25 (17084-2)

☐ **CRY WOLF** by Wilbur Smith $2.25 (11495-0)

☐ **THE BLACK SWAN** by Day Taylor $2.25 (10611-7)

☐ **PEARL** by Stirling Silliphant $2.50 (16987-9)

☐ **TILT** by James Creech III $1.95 (18534-3)

☐ **TARIFA** by Elizabeth Tebbetts Taylor............$2.25 (18546-7)

☐ **THE PROMISE** by Danielle Steel based on
a screenplay by Garry Michael White $1.95 (17079-6)

☐ **MR. HORN** by D.R. Bensen $2.25 (15194-5)

☐ **DALLAS** by Lee Raintree $2.25 (11752-6)

At your local bookstore or use this handy coupon for ordering:

Dell | **DELL BOOKS**
P.O. BOX 1000, PINEBROOK, N.J. 07058

Please send me the books I have checked above. I am enclosing $_____
(please add 35¢ per copy to cover postage and handling). Send check or money
order—no cash or C.O.D.'s. Please allow up to 8 weeks for shipment.

Mr/Mrs/Miss_____

Address_____

City_____ State/Zip_____

THE FAR CALL

by Gordon Dickson

The people and politics behind a most daring adventure—the manned exploration of Mars!

In the 1990s Jens Wylie, undersecretary for space, and members of four other nations, are planning the first manned Mars voyage. But when disaster hits, it threatens the lives of the Marsnauts and the destiny of the whole human race and only Jens Wylie knows what has to be done!

*A Quantum Science Fiction novel
from Dell $1.95*